# Corrine and the Underground Province

## by Jason Colpitts

Table of Contents

Chapter 1

Corrine's New Secret

Corrine sprang upward, high into the air, pretending that she wasn't trapped deep in the earth.

For a moment, wind whipped across her face. The feeling was both warm and cold. It felt wonderful!

Soaring clouds ran through her imagination. She flew through them. Fluffy white clouds tossed her hair about, and lifted her arms, and brushed by her face. Corrine thought she had wings! She was as free as a bird! A wide grin burst out as she soaked in the happiness.

Her heavy boots landed with a thud.

Corrine knew she was still underground, but she didn't care! Corrine was off again, bounding from one copper pot and basin to another. She dodged and spun around a hundred apple branches and tall vegetable stalks growing in each of the copper pots.

She launched upward like a dolphin out of the ocean. Corrine stretched her arms out to feel every gust. She even closed her eyes, daring to test herself. She refused to open them until just before she landed!

Suddenly, as she leapt again into the darkness an old memory popped into her mind.

Corrine remembered herself, a long time ago, crying with her arms around her knees. Corrine had created a plan – buried very deep. It was time for war, and the first part of the plan lay with two rival jumping teams. The Rockets and the Hurricanes needed to unite! They had to fight evil Madame Morticia together, and there was only one way to make it happen! But Corrine doubted herself. She felt too small, too weak, and too young!!

Then, the secret plan tumbled away into the darkness as she jumped across the spooky cavern. Corrine spun around – dazed and confused – and she almost fell! Memories flitted just beyond her fingers once again.

*What was I remembering? I hate that!* her mind screamed. *Wait! I have to compete in the tryouts! That's why I come every night. I don't remember everything, but I know this: Tell those Rockets I'm ready for the team!!!*

After leaping across the whole cavern, she finally skidded to the other side. Her heart beat furiously, she could barely keep her breath, and she was ready for more!

She turned and looked at her accomplishment. Copper pots were scattered everywhere. They were an awesome obstacle course. Running and jumping between them was difficult, especially while zig zagging through a maze of apple trees, and ducking under strings of electric lights. She took different routes every time. Never did her feet touch the same place twice.

Her cavern was like Daggers Hollow – the super dangerous cavern where the Rockets secretly trained. High above, the ceiling held thousands of sharp and windy spikes, made of stone. That's the way all the caves were. Sometimes the spikes were underfoot as well. Corrine knew she had to be careful wherever she walked. They were glorious to look at, though, made of all sorts of cool colors, reddish brown, orange, and sometimes even blue! Thankfully, they were too high to scrape her head on one!

Corrine felt so mischievous! It was very late, and the cavern was dark. Spooky shadows were everywhere. It was what she wanted, to be alone and to feel dangerous. The strings of UV lights, which they burned at nighttime, provided only a faint purple glow. In the dark, jumping was more difficult. On her last run she made only one mistake!

Beep. Beep. Beep.

Corrine's heart skipped a beat. She spied her radio, buzzing in her pocket.

*Why would he be calling at this hour?* she wondered.

She yanked it out with nervous fingers and pushed the talk button. Quietly, she whispered, "Hello?"

"Corrine, this is Jasper. Can you talk? Are you alone?"

"Are you crazy?! It's two o'clock in the morning! Of course I'm alone!" Corrine didn't want to insult an Overseer, but the question was silly.

"Listen, I have very little time. Morticia might be trying to find our signal. I am going to make some changes. Your planting ideas were very good. We are putting out your new list, but first I need to find out something. How do you know so much about planting? Corrine, are you listening?"

"Yes, I'm listening. I know these ideas are different. They're for the best. I don't know why. I don't remember things all the time," she said without an attitude.

"I understand." Jasper said, sounding like he was smiling. "Corrine, make sure you don't tell anybody else! Do you understand?"

"Yes." Her voice became more respectful.

"Okay, I have to go," he whispered. "I'll stay in touch."

Corrine pushed the talk button again. The radio shut off.

A wormy excitement started squirming in her stomach. She was so happy. An adult was listening. They were finally listening!

Her eyes filled with a whole lot of wonder and a little sneaky mischief. She was thrilled!

Without making a sound Corrine jumped up and down with glee. She danced in place – wriggling about – all while trying to keep her excitement inside.

Happily, her head turned toward the copper pots. The purple lights flashed across her eyes. This time she was determined. She wouldn't slip once! Corrine crouched down and dug her feet into the ground. She was ready to try jumping again. Audrey, her best friend, would be so proud!

*Rockets here I come!!!*

Chapter 2

The Terrible Horrible Lead Planter

The next morning, Jasper's conversation was tickling Corrine's insides.

Most of the workers who toiled in the mines or who ran the large hydraulic machines wore a sour expression when they began their work. 12-year-old Corrine never did.

She was assigned to care for the fields. Her routine included watering the plants, and pulling the weeds, and harvesting the food. It was a hard job, but she loved it.

Corrine strode proudly along another row of copper basins. The Province grew their food in these ones too, carrots and other vegetables.

She was walking down toward the front meeting area. A twisted bundle of wires made up a sort of fence around the whole place. Far ahead, more wires were bent in a high arch that made up a gateway. That was where she was going, for a meeting with all the Planters

She caught her reflection in a shiny copper basin. A big grin spread across her face. Corrine felt very pretty. She stood tall in the mirror admiring her rich dark brown skin. A set of tight-knit braids ran across her head, and she smiled as she fingered each of the dozen little buns. They were just right!

Corrine also had strong nimble fingers. Today her hands were protected by a set of heavy work gloves. These were her best ones. They were thick, white, and covered with dirt. She was ready for work and couldn't wait to see if the secret list she shared with Jasper was going to be read.

"Wipe that smile off your face!" The Lead Planter, Linda, yelled as soon as Corrine approached.

Linda was always yelling. She was always in a bad mood.

Corrine's glee flitted away. Instead, her mood dropped. She quickly folded her arms. An angry pout grew up on her face, and she pursed her lips. One side of her mouth even curled up with an attitude, and her head shimmied back and forth too.

In a way she was saying to the Lead Planter, *You ain't got nothing on me!* She knew better than to say anything out loud. She was only a worker.

Today, Linda wore faded blue overalls, a striped yellow shirt, and purple socks. Her head was a cluster of bunchiness too! Big clumps of her dirty stringy hair were tied back with a green ribbon. She looked so stupid.

What looked worse was Linda's thick pair of glasses. They didn't fit quite right. Everybody knew they used to be owned by an old man. They were big, square, and terribly thick.

They made her eyes seem beady and small. Linda had to lean forward and squint to see anything, even with the glasses on!

The Lead Planter pulled out a paper list.

While she waited, Corrine imagined that she was the Lead Planter and not that super mean headmistress, Linda. She was terrible and horrible!!! Corrine hated new rules, but this list was going to be special; Jasper promised.

Suddenly, Linda's head spun around toward Corrine. Linda had seen her attitude.

"Wipe that look off your face, and let me finish!" Linda barked.

"Yes, headmistress." Corrine snapped to attention, and then she got really mad, hot-red-beet-cheeks-mad.

Corrine did as she was told, of course. Unfolding her arms, she thrust them into the pockets of her overalls. Instead of pouting, she hid her face and kicked at small pebbles on the ground. Corrine was so embarrassed. The whole group of Pickers were watching. She knew she shouldn't have given an attitude to Linda, but Linda deserved it!

"One: Pickers need to show the Lead Planters respect!" Linda read.

Corrine frowned.

"Two: Pickers are supposed to listen!" Linda continued.

Something wasn't right.

Linda added more. "Three: Pickers are supposed to follow the rules!"

None of these rules were on Corrine's and Jasper's list. Linda was making them up. Corrine knew it.

"Four: Pickers are supposed to work!" The Lead Planter went on and on.

Linda waved her hand toward her chest. She wanted the group to step closer so she could see them better.

The group of Pickers gathered close beneath Linda's high wooden box. There were almost two hundred kids in front of the planting area, mostly orphans.

Corrine could sense that to most of them, this meeting was strange. Corrine, on the other hand, was thrilled. She kept squirming, and she couldn't stand still, not one bit!

Corrine tensed as Linda suddenly paused and shot Corrine a fiery glance. The suspicious look lasted for a whole ten seconds before the Lead Planter continued.

When she started talking again, Linda's tone suggested that she didn't like any of these new rules. She probably figured out whom the list had really come from.

"We are also going to be making a few changes to our crop placement," Linda said, tucking the list away. "We will be uprooting our tomatoes and placing them with asparagus. Also, in future plantings, lettuce will now be arranged with carrots..." She went on and on.

All the younger kids around Corrine started mumbling. Linda said "uprooting". Lead Planters never said that word. Plus, this new direction would take a lot of work. Plants would have to move from one place to another. They would risk losing good soil. Normally, it was too dangerous.

"Don't worry about her." Corrine's friend Audrey scooted behind the group of workers.

Corrine was grateful that Audrey was talking to her again. The last time she and Audrey spoke to each other it was in anger. They had an argument about Corrine's disability. Corrine had been forgetful again, and now she felt really bad about it.

Corrine didn't know why she forgot things. Other people seemed to know who they were. They could remember in the morning what their name was. Her disability was hard to understand. She forgot some things and not others. It made her soooo sad.

Corrine looked out across the green leaves. The leaves were still, like they were frozen. There was no wind down in the caverns.

No insects were left either, to do the job they once did, buzzing about from flower to flower. Now kids called Pollinators brushed the thin vegetable and fruit stems, and they used copper brushes!

Corrine hated copper!!! She didn't remember why, she just didn't like it. The sight of old corroding copper made her nose curl up and her eyes pull away. She thought her hatred for copper might be something from a long time ago.

In the past, it was said that grain grew in vast fields as far as the horizon stretched. Corrine's counselor explained it that way one time. It was the way it used to be.

Corrine started to smirk. Her fields made her happy. They covered much of the Northern Province. Maybe they didn't have vast open fields of grain, but they did have some pretty good food!

Corrine was supposed to be listening, and to do so obediently! As usual, Corrine was distracted by leaves and other things, despite the fact that Audrey kept elbowing her to pay attention.

Corrine – or "Core" as her friend Peter sometimes called her – tried to do as she was told. If the Pickers like her did a bad job, didn't pay attention, or nod Yes at the right time, Linda would give you a thick pile of oatmeal instead of meat and vegetables!

Corrine could see the large spikes of rock jutting out of the ceiling much better in the daytime lights. They were called "stalactites". More grew up from the floor here too, called "stalagmites". The spikes were beautiful. Rings of color were layered down each spike. These were a little different from the ones in her nearby cavern. The stalactites here were wider, and they looked like frozen tornados, tiny and narrow on the bottom and fat and thick at the top. They reminded her of her dreams.

*Why do I remember the way things were and then forget what I did yesterday?* She couldn't help but wonder, feeling a little mad at herself.

"Hey silly!" Audrey tried to snap Corrine's mind back. "Linda's gonna think you're not paying attention."

Corrine didn't hear Audrey. She was thinking, thinking some more, twirling a little, and smiling on the inside. No one was going to find out where the planting list came from. Her secret was huge. It wasn't like she was hiding a hairbrush in her pocket to comb Audrey's hair. Her secret was much bigger, and she was so proud of the list.

Suddenly, Corrine felt someone grab her ear and turn it painfully. She heard Audrey yelp too. Corrine neither heard Linda stop reading the list, nor come marching over.

Linda towered over them both. She was older, stronger, and much taller!

"You think this is all a joke, don't you!" Linda yelled. Her face was as red as an apple, and smoke came out of her ears. Linda looked like one of the hydraulic machines when they got really hot. They exploded with steam.

"No, headmistress!" Corrine answered her.

"How would the two of you like to scrub mold for the whole morning?"

Corrine and Audrey were too afraid to answer. Scrubbing mold was the worst!

"Huh?! I can't hear you! How would you like to scrub mold all day?!" Linda asked.

"Please no, headmistress!" Audrey squeaked out a fearful reply. No one else could have heard it.

"That's not good enough!" Linda glared at them both. "How would the two of you like..."

Corrine and Audrey dropped to their knees. "Please no! Please no!"

"...to scrub the mold..."

"Please headmistress!! We'll pay attention. We won't talk. We promise!"

"...ALL NIGHT TOO!!!"

Corrine and Audrey fell to the ground crying.

Around them, the whole crowd of kids fell silent. It was the worst punishment ever. Nobody's scrawny arms would be able to scrub for the whole morning, never mind all day!

Dozens of kids shifted awkwardly. They looked like they wanted to help, but everybody was afraid of Linda. Linda made the decisions, and most of the kids were small orphans.

Corrine and Audrey didn't have parents either. Nobody was big enough to defend Corrine or her best friend. No one would protest, and Linda must have known it. She was so mean.

Linda leaned over. As the girls sobbed, she whispered, "...and Oatmeal for a WEEK!"

Corrine hated Linda.

## Chapter 3

### Sneaking into the Hidden Building

Peter watched as Jasper snuck past the hydraulic machines.

Jasper was far away, and he clearly didn't want to be seen. He was being extremely careful. Jasper pulled his coat close, hiding his face.

Monstrous hydraulic machines were built along the edge of the Western Province. The machines were terribly loud as the hydraulics puffed, and whistled, and bumped, and banged. The whole cavern shook with noise.

There were small houses on the other side of the machines too. Peter could see orange lights from their windows. Many people lived in them. Most didn't walk on this side of the machines, however, because it was dark, too hot from steam, and this is where rocks often fell from the cavern walls. Peter figured that that was why Jasper had chosen this route. All the repair workers had gone home too.

Jasper's head swiveled back and forth. He took his time. Jasper wanted to make sure there was no one else around, but Peter was keeping a close eye on the Overseer.

Peter wasn't far behind. Peter crawled along the top of the hydraulic machines and jumped from one to the next. They

were very old, and their tops were worn and rusty. Steam
puffed out of every crack. Despite all the rumbling and
shaking Peter stayed on. He kept as low as he could.

Peter had a lot of gadgets. Sometimes, Corrine and Audrey
laughed and called them his "spy gear". Today, he brought a
whole bunch of gadgets. They were mounted behind his head,
under his hat, and inside his jacket.

Peter wore a pair of thick goggles too. His eyes looked
bulgy and huge! The goggles were funny looking with many
different lenses, buttons, and lights. The goggles even had
built in telescopes! With them, he could see Jasper far away.

Jasper had come down here two times before. That was not
like him. He was up to something, and Peter wanted to know
what. Besides, Jasper was sneaking around Peter's
neighborhood!

Peter didn't live in the Northern Province like Audrey and
Corrine. He lived in the Western Province. Everyone called it
Machine Town.

It took a long time for Jasper to come to Machine Town
today. Peter waited, hiding in air ducts for an hour. Finally,
Jasper passed by. Then, Peter carefully slid out from behind a
copper grate.

After following Jasper along the machine tops for a while,
Peter pulled a rope that was hidden under his jacket until a
wide set of metal arms popped out. At that moment, he ran a

few steps and jumped off the high machines! Fine cloth from
an old tent unfolded, and Peter sailed across the cavern.

He was wearing wings!

Peter sailed back and forth. He turned left and right. At
times, he even shot straight down! Peter looked like a giant
night owl! His wings were meant to glide, and so they couldn't
fly upward very well. Thankfully, Peter was very high when he
jumped off. Peter was clever and sneaky too. Jasper never
saw him, floating high above.

Peter glided in a circle around the machines and down to
the far edge of the cavern. The back corner was very dark. He
could barely see into the shadows.

Suddenly, he spotted something! Around a sharp bend and
a huge pile of rocks, there were groups of homes that were
ancient. These homes were dark. They had broken windows
and doors, and nobody was living in them anymore.

Also there was a small building down there, hidden on the
other side of the rocks. It was way past the hydraulic
machines. Peter thought this part of the cave had only rocks
and cliffs. He had never seen this building before. It was
carefully hidden in just the right spot.

Jasper had walked along the hydraulic machines and down
to the edge of the rocks. Now, he reached the hidden building
and its secret door. After unlocking a large chain, Jasper
pulled it off. Slowly, he turned the door handle. The door
screeched. It hadn't been opened in a long time. Again, he

looked around. He was acting very suspicious tonight. After he made sure that the sound hadn't been heard, Jasper slipped inside. With a loud bang, the heavy door slammed shut.

Peter was excited! This was turning into a great adventure!

The building was strange in another way. The door was way too big to be an ordinary door. There were deep ruts in the ground too. A long time ago, wagons must have come and gone into the hidden building. Peter began to think that people used to work here and live in these homes. Now, everything looked dusty! A long, long time ago this hidden building was well-used. Peter had to know why Jasper was sneaking in there.

Peter pulled the rope attached to his wings again. In the air he turned and then lowered gently to the ground. Without a sound, Peter landed at the very edge of the cavern.

He couldn't see at all, so he pushed a button on the thick goggles. The goggles shined a light forward. Now he could see the heavy metal door and the dirty handle.

*What could Jasper be doing?* Peter wondered.

He worried that every sound from his feet boomed like the machines. The machines were far away, but they were still loud. Nobody heard him as he sneaked over to the door.

The metal was old. It was crumbly and rusty. He put his ear against the metal and listened.

*I can't hear Jasper at all!* he thought. *How can that be?*

Digging into his backpack, Peter pulled out a bottle. The bottle had a tube coming out and brown oil inside. He squeezed the bottle. Oil sprayed all over the handle and the hinges of the door!

Slowly, Peter opened the door and held his breath! This time, it didn't make as much noise. Behind the door was a set of stone steps going down. They were very creepy and dark. Peter bravely stepped inside, down one step after another. Not wanting to get caught, Peter turned his flashlight off. Instead, he felt along the walls and listened. Peter could hear sounds ahead now, clicking and banging.

Jasper was far away tinkering with something. At the bottom of the stairs was a long hallway. It was just as dark. Peter was scared. What would he do if he got caught?!

Bravely, he snuck even closer.

The air smelled dingy and dusty.

Finally, Peter got close to the end of the hallway. Around the corner, he could see another room. This one had lots of shelves. The shelves had tubes and wires, and beakers and machine parts.

*What was this room for?* Peter couldn't imagine.

It had desks with papers, books, pens, and old computers. Clutter was everywhere! The whole room was a messy jumble.

Suddenly, Jasper stood up from behind the nearest desk!

Peter jumped!!!

Jasper had something shiny in his hand!

Peter had never seen anything like it before.

It gleamed like a bright light. It was shiny and new and was made of a metal he had never seen. Half of it was covered in a sort of plastic, like the stuff his computers at home were made of, but this plastic was different. It moved like skin, but it was a...robot arm!

Peter gasped out loud!

Jasper spun around. "Hey, who's there?!" he yelled.

Cursing himself for making so much noise, Peter grabbed the bottle of oil again. He squirted it all over the floor and ran as fast as he could! Peter ran and ran.

Peter heard Jasper try to follow him. He turned just in time to see Jasper throw the robot arm down with a clunk and jump over the desk! As soon as Jasper's feet hit the floor, he tumbled over. His legs slipped, and he skidded across the oil. He crashed into things.

From the other end of the long hall, Peter's quick glance captured it all, including a dozen books and papers spilling all over the place.

Peter knew that when Jasper finally steadied his feet, he ran too, all the way down the hall and up the stone stairs.

But Peter was gone.

By now, Peter had ducked behind the nearest hydraulic machine, and with not a second to spare! He peered out of the shadows as Jasper burst out the door.

For a whole minute, Jasper studied the darkness while Peter nervously watched. Then, after shaking his head and drying his sweaty anxious brow, Jasper slid back inside the hidden building and shut the door.

Peter breathed a sigh of relief.

*This is getting exciting,* Peter thought. *This is very, very exciting!*

## Chapter 4
### Corrine and Audrey Scrub All Night!


The two girls scrubbed and scrubbed. Their hands hurt. Their knees hurt. Their shoulders hurt. Their skin hurt. Even their eyes hurt. They scrubbed the bottom of the pots until every tiny little muscle was aching in pain.

Corrine's cavern was littered with large copper basins and small copper pots. Each large basin held a fruit tree in the center, and they grew vegetables around it. There were many, many more copper pots. Those were used to grow different kinds of potatoes, squash, and mushrooms too.

At times, foolish Pickers would miss a basin that they were supposed to water. Corrine's group was careful not to waste a drop. Once and a while it happened to some of the others, though, and sometimes a hose slipped out of their fingers. Precious liquid spilled everywhere. They got in trouble of course, but not before the mold started to grow! It grew on the bottom of every pot.

Corrine and Audrey were not allowed to leave until they washed each and every one – hundreds of them! The worst part was not the pain. It was the slimy, muckey, gooey, sticky, and very awful smelling mold. Green goo was everywhere.

A bunch of times Corrine got wet mold all over her gloves. A few times she even bumped the sliminess with her arm. Dark green sludge spread across her skin.

*Gross!* Corrine thought. *So disgusting!*

The two girls scraped it off in chunks. They peeled it off with their fingers, and they scrubbed it away with hard bristly copper brushes.

"Hey, Audrey, are you finished?" Corrine asked.

"No." A sad mousy whisper came out of her friend.

After a few minutes, it was Audrey's turn.

"Hey, Corrine, are you finished?" Audrey asked.

"No," Corrine answered, just as depressed.

The sound of scrubbing was the only thing they heard for a long time.

Corrine decided after a while that enough was enough. Her cavern was too gloomy, and they were too sad.

"Hey Audrey?" Corrine asked.

"Yes?" Audrey responded.

"Tell me about your parents. Tell me all the good things you remember."

Audrey smiled. Corrine smiled back admiring Audrey's fair skin and light brown hair. She looked like she could have been Peter's sister, except that he had light skin and dark brown hair.

"I remember so many good things," Audrey said. "My father used to tuck me into bed. We had only two books. He read one on the first night, and then he read the other on the second night. Every night he switched back and forth. I was so young I didn't really know the difference. All that mattered to me was that he was reading. I loved his voice. He was so strong. As long as he read, I felt like I could fight the whole world."

"What about your mother?"

"My mother was kind. She was warm and happy. She sang to herself when she cooked, and she tried to make me feel good all the time. I remember she told me three words, always the same three words. She said I was her sunshine, her joy, and her breath. She repeated it over and over, 'You are my sunshine, my joy, and my breath.' I loved to hear it."

"I don't remember my parents," Corrine cut her off.

"I know. Is it hard, having memory issues?"

"I don't know. Sometimes I feel bad about it, and then I forget that I felt bad. I can't seem to hang onto it all."

"Did you talk to your counselor, Maureen, about it again?"

"Yes. We talked about it. Maureen showed me pictures of my parents, but I didn't know them. I felt like I was looking at a couple of strangers."

"Did you see yourself in their faces?" Audrey was curious.

"I guess I did. It felt funny, so far away, like I wasn't looking at my dad or mom. It was hard. It's strange to me, I guess, when you *can* recall a face or a funny story. I can't. I talked about it to Maureen for a long time. She helped. She never met them herself. I think it was weird for her too, and I wonder how many times we have talked about it together."

"Five, I think." Audrey was keeping count.

Corrine always admired Audrey. Audrey was a smart girl. She wasn't as good with programming and radios as was their other friend Peter. Peter knew so much about computers. He was able to get a couple old ones running again. No one knew of course. Right now it was just a hobby. But Audrey was smart too – smart in a different kind of way. She was as sharp as a tack with people. Her eyes were always open. She noticed things about others which no one else saw.

"I'm sorry. I'm sorry we got in a fight. I'm sorry I forget things," Corrine said.

"That's okay." Audrey meant it. She knew Corrine couldn't help it.

Scrubbing mold alone in the dark made Corrine feel bad. She knew Linda would check the pots in the morning. If there was any of the icky goo left, they would get punished again. They had to finish. For now, though, nobody was watching!

Audrey looked like she had had enough too. The cave was far too gloomy.

Jumping upon one of the smaller pots, Audrey copied Linda. Audrey curled both of her hands into round circles. Then, she held her hands over her eyes to make fun of Linda's glasses.

"Hey, you!" She announced in a funny deep voice. "You two, stop talking!"

Corrine started giggling.

"How dare you talk while I'm talking!" Audrey's voice sounded rumbly, and she kept bobbing her head up and down like one of the chickens in the underground coops. "How would you like oatmeal for a month?! Wait. Where did you go? I can't see you. My glasses are too thick! Did you disappear?" Audrey started jerking her head back and forth, pretending like she couldn't see and that Corrine had just vanished.

Corrine fell over laughing on the ground. It was such a perfect performance, so, so funny. Audrey laughed too and bounced back down. She sat next to Corrine.

"Hey, let's do something fun tomorrow, something risky!" Audrey said, her eyes large and bright.

"What?" Corrine's own eyes widened with excitement.

"We could join the other kids who practice near the Falls," Audrey said.

"You mean the secret passage into Daggers Hollow? Isn't that where the gangs compete?"

Corrine was pretending not to remember stuff this time. She knew all about Daggers Hollow. Audrey didn't know she was practicing at night to get ready to compete at the Hollow. Corrine wanted to surprise her!

"...not *in* Daggers Hollow," Audrey went on. "The Falls are the other caves nearby. I think if you tried out for one of the teams you'd do really good."

"I don't know. Let's try to go to the Column tomorrow. Besides, I found something special there two days ago that I want to show you," Corrine said.

"What?!"

"I'm not telling you yet. It's a surprise."

"Okay. Fine! If we go during the day we'll have to use the back tunnel. Do you remember how well-guarded the Column is?" Audrey asked.

"Is it? I don't think I remember that. I had a dream about it a week ago. I dreamed that a whole bunch of people climbed it together."

"Hey, have you talked to your counselor about your dreams?" Audrey asked.

"I did."

"What did she say about them?"

"Maureen just sat and listened. She nodded her head a few times. I don't know. She seemed like she wanted me to feel good about them. She kept asking what other dreams I've had."

"What did you dream about this time?"

"I dreamed I worked in an infirmary, with sick people. I was a nurse. I dreamed I spent time with animals too. And I dreamed about an old scientist in a lab coat," Corrine explained.

"You've had that dream before," Audrey said simply.

"I have? I didn't know that. My counselor didn't say anything about that."

"You've definitely told her before. I remember you telling both of us several times. Was it the one in the snow?"

"In the snow...? No. Have I had a dream like that before?"

"Yes, but what was this one about?" Audrey had to know.

"This is going to sound weird." Corrine curled up on the ground. A look of embarrassment dripped down her face. "I dreamed that I was just a head!" She buried her face in her hands.

"...just a head?! That's so funny." Audrey set her at ease, sounding like she didn't want Corrine to feel embarrassed.

"I dreamed that I was just a head, and I was on a table."

"What were you doing?" Audrey yawned while she asked.

"Nothing. I was looking outside and blinking a lot."

"That's so strange." Audrey spoke while trying to stay awake.

"You're tired." Corrine's voice took on a warm tone.

"No. I'm fine. Keep talking."

"No, you're very tired! We've been working all day and night. I've seen you rubbing your arms already. You must be so sore. Why don't you go home? I'll finish. There isn't that much more to do anyway."

"Are you sure? My arms are killing me!"

"Yes. I feel fine. Don't worry about me."

Audrey stood up to go, slowly and looking like she didn't want to leave Corrine with the rest of the work. Corrine knew that if she could Audrey would have gone to sleep right there on the floor. If Corrine wasn't there to talk to, Audrey might have taken a nap already in one of the copper basins.

Corrine could see it now. All the kids would come back tomorrow to plant. Everybody would find her friend curled up and sleeping with her face in the dirt. They would jeer and poke at them both all day!

"Hey." Corrine was thinking again.

"What?" Audrey asked sleepily.

"The Column is hundreds of feet high, and it's the only way out."

"That's right," Audrey said.

"If all it does is give us a view of the storms outside, why does it need guards?"

"I don't know. You think too much."

"I'm sorry. Go to bed you nut!"

"You're the nutty one," Audrey gave her a half-hearted response.

After that, she left.

The cavern felt much quieter and a little spooky without Audrey there. The lights were dim to save electricity.

Corrine kept working. She didn't feel quite as tired. Her arms weren't as sore. They ached pretty bad, but she didn't feel like Audrey. Before she left, Audrey kept rubbing her shoulders, like her arms were about to fall off.

Corrine thought about it. She must have been pretty strong. Maybe trying out for the games was a good idea. It might be exciting to compete in the jumping. Everyone knew the Falls was the place to sneak off to, if you wanted to have any real fun...

Corrine stopped thinking.

She heard a noise across the dark fields.

Someone was out there.

Corrine's wide eyes studied the copper basins. A faint glimmer of light shone off them. She couldn't see much more.

Corrine could *hear* a person though, creeping. Corrine tried to listen. Barely able to make out the sound of footsteps, she strained to hear. Faintly, she could hear baggy clothes rustling, and then she could smell stinky sweaty feet!!!

Suddenly, there was a person behind her, super close. All Corrine could see in a glance was that the stranger had clumps of stringy white hair. She thought she saw a man's overalls too.

Then, the man quickly threw a large rough vegetable sack over Corrine's head. She kicked and screamed, but there was no one around to hear her.

Worse yet, Jasper's radio fell out of her pocket. The other person stomped hard on it. Corrine could hear it shatter into a thousand pieces. She almost cried right there!

Then, the shadowy figure forced her down to the ground. For a few seconds she could hear muffled voices, two adults talking together. Another person had joined the stringy haired man. Then, the man holding her down pushed a finger into her back. She heard a funny sound, a click and then a soft whirring.

Suddenly, Corrine felt lightheaded. She felt like her energy was draining away.

Everything went black...

## Chapter 5

### The Mysterious Snow Dream

The man that held her down reminded her of another time. She was trapped then too, a long long time ago...

Corrine was very cold.

Part of her knew she was dreaming, but there was a funny thing about her dreams. Corrine always felt like they were happening, like right now! This was the snow dream!

A storm whipped past her. Clumps of thick white snow swirled around. The wind was icy and sharp. It cut into her face and bit her skin, a bone chattering cold. Snow covered the world. There were large and small hills of snow. There were even huge spikes of ice sticking out in places.

Corrine could not see the ground. There was no dirt. There was no grass. There were no trees. There wasn't even a sky. The whole blue sky was covered by clouds, lots and lots of clouds. The clouds were making it snow. She knew that. Corrine worried that maybe it was snowing everywhere. Maybe the entire earth was snowing. That would be dreadful!

Corrine could see more. They were high above the ground. She and her friends were climbing a large mountain. The people all worked together. They were dressed warmly, and they carried a lot of rope. Her friend was there too, an old scientist. He was wonderfully nice. Sometimes he turned around and smiled at her. She liked him a lot.

Everything was going well, until suddenly, one of the ropes snapped! Everyone started shouting! People were screaming. Some of the heavy bags tumbled down the mountain, and some of the people fell too!

Corrine could hear a terrible sound from above. It was the loudest thing she ever heard. She looked up. A wave of snow was rushing down the mountain! Everyone tried to run. Corrine tried too, but she was far behind them. She ran and ran.

Snow, rocks, and ice raced toward her! Pieces of the mountain were flying everywhere!

Corrine looked around. She couldn't see. Far away, she could hear their boots crunching and ropes snapping. Her friends were in trouble!

*If only I could jump better!* she thought. *Maybe I could jump from rock to rock and help them get out of the snow. I could save everyone!!!*

She could not move fast enough to leap onto a rock. Sadly, she couldn't jump either. Quickly, her little body got tired, and her legs would not move. Then, the snow rushing down the mountain gobbled her up like a giant mouth!

The wave of snow spun her round and round. She tumbled again and again. Then Corrine fainted.

After a long time, she suddenly woke up again.

*Did I die?* she wondered.

Corrine looked around.

*I'm not dead!* she thought.

There was a gigantic shadow across the ice. It looked like the mountain. Corrine could not turn her head around to see it.

Also, her body would not move. She tried to wiggle her legs or shimmy her arms. Nothing worked. All she could do was move her eyes. Corrine studied the area around her. Her view was limited. There was heavy snow everywhere. She was stuck in it like icy glue!

She could see for miles across the whole land. Feelings of worry crept into her. She was very very worried.

Then, the wind blew really hard. It swept across the field of ice like a broom. Wind blew away all the loose snow. Soon, Corrine could see more.

It was terrible!

Her friends were clustered together at the bottom of the mountain. They were trapped! Most of their tools and snow shoes had blown away. All the boxes and bags of food were lost. They had a small tent and were taking turns climbing inside to get warm.

Corrine was very concerned about them. They were her friends. It was way too cold. She didn't think anybody was going to make it back home.

She thought hard about it and remembered what happened before everyone fell. They were faced with a tough choice. They could either walk around the mountain, or they could climb over it. If they went around, the journey would take a long time, and it was very dangerous. The old scientist and his friends thought about it for a long time. Then they chose to go up over the mountain. It was a smart choice. Corrine did not regret it...

\*\*\*

Later, Corrine found out that the wave of snow was called an avalanche. Corrine hadn't heard the word before. She decided she hated avalanches.

People shared stories about the snow sometimes. They said things used to be easier. The world was different. Everything was easy when they burned oil. After a while, smoke from the oil harmed the earth and sea. The earth fought back. It got really warm, and then it got very very cold.

People ran to hide from tornadoes which spun with daggers of ice. Chunks of sharp ice as long as a person spun around until even buildings broke apart.

There was nowhere to go but down. Tunnels were dug everywhere in the ground. People climbed down into Mother Earth like mice. The Province was one of those places. It was safe. For a while people had peace again. Life was hard

underground, and work wasn't easy, but they were alive and
very grateful.

No one from that time was around anymore. Nobody
remembered before the storms, before the sky filled with
clouds and lightning, and before the long winters began.

A long time ago, as the story went, different Provinces used
radios to talk to each other. It was too cold to go outside, and
everybody was afraid of the tornadoes. Then, their radios
grew old and broke. Now, none of the Provinces spoke to each
other. No one knew if any other people were still out there.

Corrine's Province, called NewTown, felt like they
were pretty lucky. Their Province had not only
survived, but they had grown. Now almost three
thousand people filled the many caverns!

\*\*\*

*Why did my friends leave the Province? Why did
they climb the mountain? We were safe,* she
wondered, and then her head snapped to. *This must be
one of my craziest dreams!!!*

Corrine remembered the people who shared the tent. It
was hard to see through the ice storm. Once and a while, the
wind blew just right, and she could see the scientist from the
lab.

He had on a heavy winter coat. The coat was puffy, and it looked warm. Still, the wind was harsh. He looked like he was getting just as cold as the others.

Corrine watched as the old man stepped out of the tent and stared at the storm. He looked out at the mountain. He looked at the trail of broken tools. He also looked at Corrine. The distance between them was massive. His gaze managed to find her though.

Here she was, so far away, and pinned up against the side of the mountain. The avalanche had stopped. All the snow, which moved so fast a little while ago, was now frozen. She looked around. Everything around Corrine was solid, a block of snow and ice.

The old scientist frowned. She was too far away.

*Help us!* She yelled on the inside. *We need help.*

Corrine wished he could save her. She wished the group of people would be able to make the trip back home. Knowing that they couldn't, Corrine started to cry. She wished she was dreaming. She wished she would wake up.

*Help us!* She yelled inwardly again. *We need help.*

Instead, she wished the others could receive help. Desperately, she hoped they would get saved.

Corrine kept thinking and thinking about the idea. They needed help. Was anybody out there who could?

*Help us! We need help.*

## Chapter 6

### Finding a Strange Purple Flower

Corrine awoke with a start!

She felt frumpy, bumpy, lumpy, and altogether grumpy!!!

"Oh, no!" Audrey screamed. "You forgot again?!"

"What happened?" Corrine asked with a groggy voice.
"Where am I? Who are you? Can you help us? We need
help!" She thought she was still dreaming.

Corrine lay on a strange bed. She was in a strange house,
and now, she was talking to a very strange person.

"Oh my goodness! Oh my goodness! This is *sooo* bad!"
Audrey's voice was shrill. She took in a deep breath and
shouted as fast as she could, "Okay. Okay! I've got this! You
live here. This is your bed. Your name is Corrine. I'm your
best friend!! My name is Audrey. Jumping tryouts are
tomorrow! You wanted to go to the Column! And the SHIFT
CHANGES IN TWENTY MINUTES!!!"

Audrey's arms were crossed, and she stood in the middle
of the room tapping her foot loudly. She glared at Corrine in
such an angry way, Corrine thought that electricity was about
to shoot out of Audrey's eyes and burn the sheets off Corrine's
bed!

"Okay. Okay! I'm hurrying!!!" Corrine said as she leapt out of bed and ran into the bathroom.

As fast as she could, Corrine threw on her overalls and sneakers.

"Hurry up, you slowpoke! Do you want the guards to catch us?!" Audrey demanded, her voice sounding muffled from the other side of the door.

It was hard to move in the teensy tiny bathroom. Most people only had a small bathroom, like Corrine's. Only full families were allowed to live in the double sized homes! Moms and dads got to have two whole rooms, but no matter what everybody's house was small, and still made of copper. Corrine hated copper! She turned her nose up!

"Okay! I'm ready!" Corrine shouted.

Corrine jumped out of the bathroom, and the two girls flew out the door. Audrey grabbed her by the hand and sprinted forward.

Audrey pulled her along so fast. The two friends bumped into wash barrels and ducked under clotheslines. Pants, shirts, and even stinky socks hung from everywhere. The girls tried hard not to get hit in the face!

Everyone was curious about the girls. The twosome darted in and out of tiny yards. They leapt off steps and jumped over fences.

One house after another whizzed by in a blur! Dogs barked. Cats screamed and ran for cover. A lot of people turned to scold them, but the girls were gone in a flash! They ran and ran, and ran some more!

They didn't stop to say hello to anybody.

Besides, everybody else looked dreadful!

Most of the Province worked in a dirty environment. They either mined for copper, coal, tried to find good dirt, or dug more caverns to live in. Some helped to care for chickens and pigs. Others scrubbed pots in the kitchens. Most adults had dirty clothes. Dirty, dirty, dirt was everywhere, and on top of the dirt was a lot of gooey dust!!! Everyone had greasy faces and sooty hair!

Today, the girls ran like lightning. It was the best run they ever had. After five minutes, they reached the edge of a special secret tunnel.

Many caverns were connected by these tunnels. Some of the tunnels were used to walk back and forth to different parts of the Province. Others had large pipes, like this one. The pipes were always made of copp...Corrine squeezed her eyes shut. She didn't want to think about copper this time!!! The copper pipes were almost entirely green. Nasty gross water dripped off them!

This secret tunnel was the only way to sneak over to the Column. An adult couldn't squeeze under the pipes like Audrey and Corrine could. The two girls crawled on their knees for a while. Then they stood and scooted behind the biggest one.

Corrine knew they were getting close to the Column when Audrey whispered loudly, "Shhh!"

Both guards near the Column were going to change shifts soon. The girls waited.

After what felt like forever, the two guards in black uniforms began to leave. The guards walked away down a long metal hallway which had a metal ceiling to keep the guards safe from falling rocks. Their walking was so loud, Corrine felt like she could hear them a mile away. The metal hallway echoed every sound. She knew exactly when the guards were far away, and often they spent time down the other end, talking to new guards.

For about ten minutes the girls would be alone. Slowly, Corrine and Audrey slipped into another smaller cavern.

Then, they looked up.

The Column rose high above them. It was dark and scary, like a wide hole in the ceiling. The hole went up and up. There were sharp digging marks on the walls of the cavern below the Column and all around Corrine and Audrey.

A long time ago, in the time of their grandparents, people dug from the earth above down into the Province and created it. Everyone said they were lucky to find these caverns.

The girls squinted. The hole above them wasn't very straight, but if you stood in the right spot, you could see all the way to the top. The Column was longer and higher than the whole tunnel they just climbed through! It was longer and higher than every tunnel in the whole Province!

Way at the top they could see massive storms. Lightning flashed! Thunder boomed. Dark clouds swirled past the top. It was very very scary.

The Column was dangerous too. Pieces of stones often tumbled down. They could hit you in the head, and that would really hurt! Sometimes the ground shook too. Rocks and dirt rained down like a waterfall!

Audrey was looking with her eyes wide open.

"I bet with enough practice, you could jump up the whole Column. Look at how many footholds there are," Audrey said.

"No way. I don't think anybody could make that many jumps in a row," Corrine said, shaking her head no.

"Do you think Aaron could do it?"

Corrine shrugged. That was a hard question. He was the head of the Rockets, after all.

Corrine was excited about the tryouts tomorrow.

Imagine! Almost a hundred kids would be jumping and tumbling through the obstacle course. There were cones, platforms, and bars to dodge, and leap from, and duck under. It was hard! Only one kid would make the team! Right now, there were nine teenagers, full-on Rockets, that were part of the team. They had awesome jumping skills. There were different types of jumping. Some kids flipped better. Others jumped higher or farther, but the Rockets could do all three at once.

After tryouts, the winner would be invited to train in Daggers Hollow.

Some said that spooky Mortimer, Morticia's brother, haunted those caves, and because of the creepy stories, few dared to explore deep into it.

The Rockets knew the whole cavern, however! They had no fear! They always invited the winner to the deepest one. That's where the real jumping began.

There were whispers that Daggers Hollow had no bottom. The kids said that if you fell, no one would ever see you, ever again. Aaron made the jumps over fifty times!

*He's so handsome,* Corrine thought, trying to act normal. She didn't want anyone to know, even Audrey.

Corrine looked up and started staring in space. Audrey laughed.

Corrine was trying to think about how to answer. Most of the time, Corrine did so much thinking, she ended up not saying anything! Adults found it frustrating. Audrey always treated Corrine's habits like they were adorable! Corrine appreciated that. Audrey seemed to know what Corrine was thinking. Corrine knew that she got a funny look in her eye every time Aaron's name was brought up.

Instead of answering, Corrine hid her face. It was turning red. Instead, she grabbed Audrey's arm and changed the subject.

"Hey," Corrine said, "Do you remember that I told you I found something?"

"Of course I do!" Audrey answered.

"Come here. It's in the darkest corner."

"We have to hurry! We're gonna get caught! Do you know how much trouble we'll get into? They'll throw us in the dungeons with creepy Mortimer!"

"He's not real, Audrey. He's just a bunch of stories. Adults use them to scare little children. Forget about him. This is special. I need you to see it. It's so pretty."

"Pretty?" Audrey was very curious.

"I came here the other day."

"You remember coming here?" Audrey was surprised.

Corrine knew her disability was changing. When she forgot before, it took weeks to remember. Now her memory was coming back faster and faster.

"I know. It's weird. An hour ago I couldn't tell you my name. Now I remember seeing the flower."

"THE WHAT?!" Audrey screamed.

Corrine jumped and put both hands over Audrey's mouth. They panicked and looked around. The guards were very far away and still talking. The two girls breathed a sigh of relief.

"You saw what?!" Audrey whispered like she was shouting. She was so excited.

They had only five minutes left. Sneaking to the edge of the small cave, they walked toward the darkest corner. As they got close, something changed.

For a few seconds, sunlight bounced off the rocks and down the Column. It wasn't very strong because of the storms outside, but it was just bright enough. The light shined in such a pretty way. It moved like a flashlight beam along the wall and across the floor. It wouldn't last long.

For only a minute the corner got warm and bright. The shadows were gone. They could see a lot of muddy dirt and dripping water. And there on the furthest rockshelf was a beautiful flower.

Audrey's mouth fell open. The fields they worked in had a lot of flowers. There were yellow ones and orange ones. Neither had ever seen a flower like this! It was long, purple, and had light streaks of yellow down the middle of each petal.

"It's so, so pretty!" Audrey whispered as loud as she could.

"I found it here the other day. The guards have never seen it. I'm not surprised. They always have their backs to this Corner, and the sunbeam comes only when they're gone. I studied the Column, when the light came down. That poor flower only gets a few minutes of light every day..."

"What are you saying?"

"Let's take it home. I have a pot, and we can get some water. I think it would have a better chance to live."

"We have to go soon, Corrine! I think the guards are finished talking."

"No," Corrine said. "It may have sprouted here, but it can't live long. If someone is in trouble, and if we can help, we HAVE to help! Besides, there's something important about this plant."

"What?" Audrey whispered as her eyes opened wide in wonder.

"I don't know, I can't remember. There's just something important about it," Corrine said.

"Okay, but scoop it out fast!!! They're coming up the hall."

The guard's boots banged a lot as they walked up the metal flooring.

Quickly, Corrine dug her hands down into the dirt. This time the muddy slimy dirt didn't bother her. She knew she was doing a good thing.

"Hey you!" one of the guards barked a command. "Stop right there!"

Both guards had a blast stick. One of them pushed a button on his stick. A large ball of green slime-energy shot out. His stick made a weird noise, like the way a rotten apple sounds when you squish it in your fingers, but much louder. The green ball flew toward the girls and just missed. In a burst of goo, its energy splattered all over the place. The cavern lit up with an eerie dark green color.

Corrine was happy she grabbed the flower. It surely would have been ruined!

The girls took in a deep breath and fled. Rushing as fast as they could, they ran back to the secret tunnel behind the pipes, and just in time. As they slid to safety, two guards charged around the corner.

Scampering like little mice, Corrine and Audrey darted away from the Column, through the entire dark tunnel, and under and between all the icky pipes.

Then, and only then, did they burst into giggles.

*How did we get away with it?!* Corrine wondered.

Corrine knew they couldn't stay long, but the more they looked at each other, the more they laughed. Corrine clutched the flower safely, as her whole body shook with glee! They giggled so hard; they couldn't even stand!

Both slid down to the ground under a large pipe.

They had the flower!

Corrine was so happy.

Chapter 7

Corrine Remembers a Message

After that morning, Corrine had to work in the fields.

Most of the orphans were quiet. The new rules were better, but hard. There was so much replanting to do. Also, they were afraid of Linda. Everyone knew that yesterday's punishment was super hard!

Linda left the twosome alone, for now. That was because the pots looked soooo good. The two girls did a really good job last night. Audrey kept rubbing her shoulders. She was still very sore.

Every once and awhile, Corrine would wink or wave. Audrey needed support. She had energy earlier this morning when they ran to the Column. Now it was gone. Audrey tried to smile back, but she was too tired. The work last night and the adventure this morning drained them both.

After a long time, Audrey took a water break. Before taking a big sip, she smiled weakly and gurgled with water still in her mouth, "Hey, where did you hide the flower?"

"I put it on the windowsill," Corrine answered.

Audrey spit her water out in a giant spray! "What?! You put it right in the window?!"

"Relax silly! It's behind the curtains. I put it right next to my wood carving, you know, the dolphin I had when we first met. I tucked it away, just right."

"Oh my goodness! I thought someone was going to find out," Audrey said.

"No. I put it off to the side, in a cup. The other day I borrowed some dirt from the copper pot down there." Corrine pointed.

Audrey looked over. "I always thought that one had too much dirt."

"That's because I moved one spoonful to it every day."

"You did?!" Audrey's face wrinkled strangely.

"How else was I supposed to get the dirt? I've wanted to plant something at home for a long time."

"That's so weird!" Audrey said with wonder, while wrinkling her eyebrows and rubbing her chin.

"Why?" It was Corrine's turn to wrinkle her face. "The flower is special. It means something."

"Why did you save dirt for a flower you hadn't seen yet? You only found it three days ago."

"Yes, but I knew. I've been waiting for it. Something special is about to happen, and the flower is the key. I can't explain why. When I found the flower, I stared at it all night. The purple and yellow petals, the green leaves, the soft way it moved, it all means something."

"You stayed under the Column all night?" Audrey sounded stunned. She was barely able to ask the question.

"I snuck into the corner when the guards changed shifts. I sat in the dark behind the flower for hours. When they switched positions again, I left."

"How do you remember all that?!" Audrey almost started shouting. She wasn't mad. Her voice perked up with excitement! "This morning you gave me that look, you know, the one where you can't remember your name. I had to introduce myself again. When you forget, you lose almost everything. You don't always remember jumping. You don't remember either the games, Linda, Peter, or me. You don't always know how to get to the fields. But do you know that there's one thing you never ever forget? Not even once?"

"What?" Corrine whispered.

"You never forget how to plant. Sometimes I have to make you breakfast, because you don't remember how. I show you where your work clothes are. Then I lead you to work by the hand. You never remember the route. But once you're in the fields, you take over planting, seeding, and watering like you never left. That's why it's so weird. You don't remember what we did yesterday, but you remembered the flower from three days ago. You knew what to do with it as soon as you saw it. You already had the dirt, and you took care of it."

Corrine grew quiet. She was embarrassed. She didn't know how much Audrey did for her every day. In a soft tone, she said, "You're such a good friend."

"You always help me, Corrine. We're friends. That's what friends do. They help each other when they're feeling down. You winked at me earlier when I was feeling sore and sad. You're a good friend too, Corrine."

"Thanks, Audrey." Corrine was happy. Audrey understood her. She was a very good friend.

Suddenly, they turned their heads. The large leaves near them wiggled and bounced about. The girls were caught off guard. It was hard to see through all the green plant leaves. At first, the wiggling leaves were far away, then they were closer and closer. Something was creeping up on them! Then, the nearby leaves made a loud rustling noise.

Both girls shrieked as Peter's head popped out of all the greenery! He looked like a bug. His giant glasses made his eyes look huge!

"Peter!" Audrey shouted. "Are you sneaking up on us? You're supposed to be working!"

"You scared us half to death! What are you doing here?" Corrine agreed.

"Hi, Audrey. Hi, Core. I have something to tell you!" Peter yelled back. "This is too important! The machines will be just fine!"

Peter worked with older hydraulic machines, the ones that were falling apart. A lot of men had forgotten how to fix them. Peter was very smart. He was good with machines and other things. He often worked with the men in the Province to get the hydraulics running again. It was his job, and he would get in big trouble if the older men in Machine Town found out he snuck away.

"Corrine found something too!" Audrey happily added.

Peter was too excited to listen. "I found an arm. I mean, it was like an arm, but it wasn't! It was from a ROBOT!"

"A ROBOT!!!" Both girls screamed.

Quickly, Peter pressed both of his hands onto their faces, to keep Corrine and Audrey from being heard. Instead, the two girls squirted out a whole bunch of weird squeaks! Their faces filled with air, and they looked like a couple teapots ready to explode!

As soon as Peter let go, Corrine started rambling, "What do you mean, a robot? I read about them in your books. They were big clunky things. A lot of people used them before the Province existed. You saw one?"

"Not a whole one, Core," Peter answered. "It was more like a hand, a very big hand, and part of an arm."

"That's so cool!" Corrine said with glee. "Where did you find it?"

"I followed my Overseer. He's been acting weird. You remember, right? Corrine, didn't you talk to him when you came to visit? You were in the Center together. His name was Jasper."

"No Peter," Audrey answered for her. "She forgot again."

"I'm sorry Peter. His name sounds important. I know I was supposed to remember something, but I can't," Corrine admitted.

"I heard you from far away." Peter pointed at the edges of his glasses. There was a funny dish stuck to the side. It had a microphone in the middle and some wires that were tucked behind his ears. He smirked. "I'm sorry I spied on you, but he has been sneaking around a lot."

"What did we talk about?" Corrine asked.

"You told him you had new ideas about how to plant. You were driving him crazy, twirling and all!" Peter explained.

"Those were your ideas!" Audrey was very surprised. "I should have known. They were the best planting ideas I've ever heard of!"

"You really think so?!" Corrine happily squealed.

"Jasper has been collecting all kinds of books," Peter continued. "He's been reading a lot about something. I don't know what yet. He's been walking around the Province a ton too. He's gone to all the different Sectors, and he takes notes. When he thinks no one is looking, he draws pictures of each place. He's been looking for something. Yesterday, I think he found it."

"What did he find?" Audrey asked.

Peter didn't have a chance to answer. As fast as he could he ducked back into the leaves.

"I'll tell you later. Bye, Audrey. Bye, Core," he whispered from inside the jungle of big leaves. "Here comes Linda."

Just like he said, Linda came marching over. The leaves shook a bit as Peter snuck away. The girls tried to pay attention to Linda so she didn't get suspicious.

"Your water break is taking too long! Audrey, get back to work!" their Lead Planter barked.

Linda just had to be mean.

"Yes, Lead Planter!" Audrey obeyed. Redness filled her cheeks.

There was no attitude from either girl today. They didn't want to be punished again.

Once Audrey ran down to the far edge of the field, Linda turned back to Corrine.

"Your Counselor wants to talk to you."

"Why?" Corrine asked politely.

"I don't know why! Does it matter? She wants you, and you have to go. Now!" Linda ordered.

Corrine started to leave, and then she stopped to speak. "You don't have to yell, you know!" Corrine knew she had an attitude again, but she didn't care.

Other kids nearby froze and stared. Their mouths dropped open. Nobody dared to yell at a Lead Planter.

"What did you say?!" Linda grabbed Corrine's overalls and pulled her close.

"We know you have a hard job!" Corrine yelled with an angry pout. "It isn't easy being the Lead Planter. We respect you, and I don't know why, but we like you! We want to listen, but it's hard sometimes. This work is hard. My hands hurt. My knees hurt. We don't always want to work. If you asked nicely and didn't yell, we would listen. I promise you, we would listen. And she told me! She was sick. She told me!!! She said, 'Tell her. Tell her I love her. Tell Linda how much she meant to me!!!'"

Linda stopped. Clearly, no one ever spoke to her like this.

"Who?" Linda whispered while starting to cry. "Who told you?"

Corrine reached out and pulled Linda's hands off her overalls.

Corrine started crying too. Her bottom lip began quivering. "Do you know how hard this is for me?" she stammered. "I DON'T REMEMBER ANYTHING!!!"

Linda stood there speechless. The other kids were all silent. Audrey was watching from far away. She was gasping too.

Corrine turned away and ran, too afraid of what Linda would say next. Wiping her face, she skittered off.

## Chapter 8

## An Adventure into the Mecca!


The Mecca was incredible! It was the center of the whole Province. Everyone went there. People bought food. They bought clothes and tools too. On the weekend, they even played music and games! Laughing is amazing to listen to.

The Mecca also smelled good. Scrumptious cinnamon from apples danced past Corrine's nose.

All the latest clothes were on display in wooden shops. The booths had scarves, shoes, and beautiful new shirts. They were so pretty! Corrine and Audrey loved to come here.

One of the best things about the Mecca was that it was clean. There was no mine soot anywhere! Workers swept, and dusted, and washed everything. The wooden beams were cut smooth, and the copper here was shiny and new.

Corrine liked it so much, she thought she might change her feelings about copper!

*No!* she stammered on the inside, while stomping on the outside as she journeyed toward the Mecca and her counselor's building. *I'm too upset! I still hate copper!*

The Mecca had huge buildings for all the Overseers. Most people called the inner part "The Center". Only important people went there. They made hard choices to help the

Province. The Overseer's meetings were very long and must have been so boring! The Overseers talked about everything. They talked about the pipes and the hydraulic machines. They talked about the caves and the digging. They had many, many meetings!

*Boring! Boring! Boring!* Corrine thought as she rolled her angry eyes.

The Province Overseers met there too. The highest Overseer was Madame Morticia. She ruled the whole Province with an iron fist. She shared her building with General Rodney – the Captain of the Guards.

Some people said Morticia had a brother too, Mortimer. Corrine thought that if Madame Morticia actually had a brother, he couldn't have been any creepier than her!

Madame Morticia was very strange-looking, tall and skinny. Her hair was extra ugly, dry and stringy. It was black with white streaks, and she tied it in an awful bun!

*What a spooky lady!* Corrine thought. *Anyone who wears an ugly bun can't be trusted! She would probably side with Linda too!*

Today, she wasn't here to shop. Corrine was furious about the fight she had with Linda, and she couldn't put all her feelings into words. Linda was so incredibly awful! She knew Linda would make her pay for mouthing off. Corrine didn't want to go back to the fields, ever again.

Most of the kids did as they were told. They were all so fearful. Even Audrey was afraid of Linda. Corrine was afraid too, but not enough to stop fighting! Linda was wrong!

Corrine stormed through the Mecca with her arms folded. She charged like a windstorm through the whole center, that is, if the Province had windstorms!

After a few minutes, Corrine marched up to a white building. It had pretty doors made of apple wood.

On the walls inside, there were paintings and carvings. Clean water poured from a pretty fountain. The Counselors moved these things around all the time. The pictures were always in a different place.

This was a special building. Sometimes people got into arguments with each other. They came here to talk about it, and to make peace. It was nice.

Corrine started to feel funny as soon as she walked in. It was an odd feeling, itchy and zingy at the same time! It happened when she looked over at a beautiful silver table.

*Where did the silver come from?* she wondered.

Corrine came here many times, but she was never dizzy before! This time, she felt like she had twirled on a chair for the whole day. Suddenly, she felt like the whole room was spinning! Everything she saw got fuzzy.

Corrine found herself wide awake and still falling into a dream.

The paintings, the door, the wall, and even the silver table faded from her eyes...

\*\*\*

Now, she could see the sky. Her head was on a table, just her head! That was so weird! Corrine felt very peaceful. She was looking out of a window. There were grey clouds in the distance. The land outside was beautiful. There were trees everywhere. Trees! All kinds of them!

Behind Corrine, people were yelling and moving around quickly. Everyone was taking a big trip. This would not be a vacation! Everyone had to run away.

A small group was arguing about Corrine, like she wasn't even there! Someone from the group said that Corrine had to stay behind. She would be left alone! That would be very very scary! But another person, a man, said no. He said she was special, and he sounded nice. Corrine was grateful that they finally agreed with the nice man.

After that, the whole group talked about a storm. The nice man said it was coming soon. Everything was about to get very cold. He was right. Ice was going to kill all the trees...

*"Corrine?"*

...Corrine was still dreaming, and she found herself sitting on a silver table. It was the same table as the one in the Province!

Corrine was just a head without her body. Suddenly, a person made sure to grab her head. They ran down some stairs while cradling Corrine's head carefully, and bolted out the door.

From far away, Corrine could see the place they were just in. People called it the "Dome". It was round, like a huge bowl and was made of silver and glass.

Then Corrine saw the worst part! There was a terrible storm on the edge of the sky. The ice tornados looked black! Under the storm, the dome was very small. Dark gusts of wind and snow spun toward them. It looked terrible!

In the parking lot, the group rushed into a small truck. People were shouting and running by. Many were carrying tables and chairs out of the building. All sorts of machines were tied on big trucks with ropes. It was scary!

Corrine was placed on a truck seat between the adults. She started to cry. Everyone looked at her oddly. They didn't know she *could* cry.

Then, a whole bunch of other trucks and cars joined them. There were so many people. Everyone was frightened. All together they drove off, down the driveway, and onto a wide road.

*"Corrine?" The voice sounded like it was far away. This person wasn't part of the dream. Corrine knew she had to wake up.*

Somehow she couldn't.

Corrine dreamed about the storm. It had long fingers.
They froze and broke everything they touched. The wind was
so strong. Their truck bounced and shook. They had to drive
fast, away from the Dome and the whole Circle of Science, to
get away. Seconds later, the silver building got eaten by the
storm. Glass went everywhere!

And then...and then...

***

"Corrine, honey?" Corrine's Counselor, Maureen, gently put a
hand on her shoulder. "Are you okay dear?"

"Yes, Maureen. I'm okay." Corrine snapped out of the
dream and remembered where she was standing.

They were still in the front room of the nice white building.
The paintings and wood carvings were all around her again.

*That was weird!* she thought. *I've never had a dream
standing up before!!!*

Corrine's Counselor was short, and she had a round face.
Whenever Maureen got embarrassed or mad, her cheeks
turned bright pink! She was dressed nicely too. She had a
dark blue skirt and a light blue shirt. Corrine thought that
Maureen was pretty and wonderfully wonderful!

"Do you like our new table?" Maureen asked. "We found it
in a storeroom. It was very dirty. Look how polished it is
now! Well, why don't we go down to my office."

"Okay," Corrine answered. "That sounds good. Did you know that I've seen that table before?"

"You have?" Maureen smiled. "Tell me about it, silly girl. Did you have another dream?"

"Yes. This one was crazy!" Corrine said with a wide grin. "I dreamed that I was in a round building. It was called the Dome!"

"A dome? What a funny word!" Maureen laughed.

They walked together and talked about the strange dream. Corrine told her everything. She told Maureen why she was so mad. She told her about Linda. She even told her about forgetting this morning and how Audrey helped her. Corrine and Maureen talked for a long time. Corrine felt like they were good friends.

Halfway through talking, though, Maureen asked Corrine a hard question.

"Corrine," she said, very serious, "I know you would never lie to me. Did you and Audrey go to the Column today?"

That's why Maureen wanted to see her! Corrine almost fell off her chair! She sunk down and folded her arms again, as frustrated as could be!!! Corrine didn't like getting caught. Her heart beat very fast. She didn't want to lie. Lying is terrible. Instead, Corrine gulped loudly. She looked up at Maureen, and Maureen looked back and waited.

Corrine answered quietly, "Yes, Counselor." It was the right thing to say.

"Corrine, you know the Column is off limits," Maureen said sternly. "It's very dangerous. You and Audrey could have gotten hurt. Do you understand? The Guards spotted a couple intruders this morning. They said one of them had light skin, and the other had dark skin. I knew it was you two right away. I don't know what we're going to do, Corrine. That was a very bad thing to do. Why did you go to the Column?"

"I wanted to look up and see the storms. I wish they would go away forever!"

"The storms are never going away, Corrine. We have to be careful. Outside is dangerous. This earth will never be the same. Do you know what happened the last time people left?"

"No," Corrine said while she pouted.

"It was a long time ago. Most of them died. Madame Morticia's parents passed away then. They froze out on the ice. Do you understand why we need to protect the Column? She does not want anyone to go outside and get hurt."

"Yes, but your parents didn't die! I had a dream about them once, outside on the ice, and I helped them return home."

"I know." Maureen smiled. "We've talked about that story before. I told you about my parents. I'm not surprised you had a funny dream after that."

"I remember what you said." Corrine tried to be good. "Dreams are just dreams. We can't go around pretending they're real. If people left, they wouldn't live very long. Everybody knows that."

Corrine shuffled her feet. Her voice was growing weaker and weaker.

"And," Maureen leaned forward and asked, "what are you supposed to remember?"

"I have to keep my feet underground," Corrine answered. She folded her arms tight and wouldn't look at Maureen.

"Okay," Maureen said kindly. "I trust that you'll remember this for the future. We are happy and safe down here. You have a good home. We'll talk about this more next week."

"Okay. Thank you, Counselor." Corrine breathed a sigh of relief. Even though her shoulders hung low, she could have been in much more trouble. Thankfully, Maureen didn't ask about the flower!

After that Maureen let her leave.

Corrine walked slowly out of Maureen's room. She passed the paintings and beautiful wood carvings. There was a name carved into the bottom of each carving: Ethyl. Ethyl must have been very good at carving. Maureen had at least a hundred!

After that, Corrine passed the gurgling water fountain. Then she stopped. One of the carvings caught her eye. Someone had carved a flower and then painted it orange. She knew it was a squash flower. The wood carving was nice.

When she saw it, Corrine remembered two things. First, the flower she found was not like this one. Hers would never grow into a piece of fruit. It would never become a vegetable. Her purple flower was just a flower. Its only job was to be beautiful, and it was!

Second, she remembered its name. It was called an Iris.

\*\*\*

After Corrine left, Maureen picked up the phone.

"Hello? Madame Morticia?" she asked.

"Yes, Maureen. I'm here. Those *were* the two girls at the Column, right?" Madame Morticia asked with a strict tone. Her voice sounded like an old piece of wood, dry and cracky.

"Yes. It was Corrine and Audrey." Maureen sadly shook her head.

"Drat. What about the Dreams?" Morticia asked.

Maureen answered, "She's having more. Corrine has them almost every day now."

"What about the test?"

"The table? I put the silver table in the foyer, and she started dreaming right away. Corrine stared at it for almost thirty minutes. I don't think she knew how long it was. I snapped her awake. Then she told me she had a dream about a dome."

"Maureen, you know this is getting dangerous. As long as they're friends, Audrey is in danger. More than that. The whole Province is in danger. I understand the gang tryouts are soon?"

"Yes, I've been able to get a few snippets from some of the other kids. I think they're tomorrow," Maureen sighed.

Maureen knew what Morticia was thinking. She certainly didn't like it, but Madame Morticia was the head of the Province. And she had ways of silencing a person who didn't cooperate.

"This whole thing is getting out of control. We need to bring these games to an end. Besides, I heard the Rockets are planning something big. That kid, Cutter, he wants to get even! Tell the kids to keep their eyes open. Also, call Jasper. I have a feeling he might be close to Corrine. I'll see what he knows. See if you can get him down here. Maureen, you can't keep protecting her. We might have to shut the whole thing down, Corrine, the tryouts, the Rockets, everything," Morticia said with a super creepy tone.

"I understand, Madame. It's very sad, but it'll have to be done. Corrine is too dangerous."

## Chapter 9
## The Rocket's Tryout


Corrine was sad after meeting with Maureen, but the next morning she woke up with squirmy wormy nerves! Tryouts were today!!! She was soooo excited.

Audrey would be here soon! Before Corrine could even change her pajamas, her door flung open.

"Hurry up, you crazy slowpoke!" Audrey shouted, all smiles.

"I'm coming! I'm coming!" Corrine spit out an answer.

Corrine leapt off the bed and ran into the bathroom. She needed all the help she could get. In a few seconds she was out like a flash. Corrine wore her favorite running suit. It was pink and purple.

After eating, they ran as fast as they could.

The tryouts were held at an old abandoned scrapyard. The scrapyard was way far away, and they had to walk for almost a mile through abandoned tunnels. The whole Province threw junky metal and old broken machines into the scrapyard. It was gigantic. There was a lot of trash everywhere, and the scrapyard had many secret ways through the piles of rubble.

At the edge of the scrapyard, kids from all over the Province joined in a line. Audrey and Corrine snickered and giggled.

They could not keep their excitement inside. The other kids looked like they were ready to jump. One by one they were led through a secret path between the trash piles.

They had to duck under sharp metal spikes and jagged gears. Nasty oily and rusty metal was everywhere. Most of the broken machines had turned greenish.

*Yuck!* Corrine thought. *Copper!*

"Gross!" Audrey announced, somehow picking Corrine's feelings right out of her head.

It was hard to see. The secret path was long. Torches lined the way, and the pathway looked really cool and a tad frightening.

Finally, the kids walked into a hidden clearing. The clearing was wide and impossible to find inside the giant scrapyard. There were a whole bunch of firelights setup in a circle. It looked very cool!

Aaron stood up on a high platform. He was so handsome. Aaron was tall. He had dark skin too, but not dark as Corrine's. He had dark brown hair and brown eyes. His family in the old world was Spanish. His running suit was red. Someone had carefully sewn yellow bolts of electricity onto his suit. Aaron also had lots of muscles.

Corrine squealed inside, and Audrey squealed out loud! Most of the girls who worked in the fields talked about Aaron. They all squealed too!

His platform was high above a tough obstacle course. Aaron looked back and forth.

"Are you ready to jump?!" he shouted.

The kids screamed as loud as they could. Red fire breathed life into the crowd.

"I'm sorry. What???" Aaron pretended like he couldn't hear them.

This time they grabbed junk from the edge of the clearing. Everybody banged metal bars together and kicked drums. All kinds of screaming and noise exploded!

Corrine covered her ears. Audrey jumped up and down. She looked at Corrine while screaming, laughing, and then screaming some more.

"That's what I'm talking about!!!" Aaron continued. "Today we have a special course for you. Fifty of you applied, five will make it into the finals, and only ONE of you will be chosen! If you are good enough, you, me, and my eight other Rockets, will dare to challenge our rivals, the Hurricanes! Who of you is brave enough? Which of you is skillful enough? Who of you is fast enough... to... try... the... GAUNTLET!!!"

Everyone cheered. Almost all of the kids bounced up and down.

The rest of the Rockets, Aaron's team, circled around the group. They wore red running suits too. Carefully, they watched the obstacle course. Each of them had sharp eyes.

No one trying out would be able to make a mistake. If you fell and hit the sand below, it was all over!

Corrine shivered. Those squirmy worms in her belly wouldn't be quiet. She didn't jump up and down with the others. She didn't scream along. Even when Audrey grabbed her arm and tried bouncing together, Corrine wouldn't budge. She was too nervous!

To be fair, one of the Rockets, a girl, got up first. This girl was tall, and she had almond shaped eyes. She was a beautiful Asian. The tall girl took in a deep breath, and then she started leaping. The gauntlet looked so simple when she did it. She flipped, spun, and even danced! She looked like a beautiful Asian poem. This girl was so fast. In a minute she landed on the other side.

Corrine knew it really wasn't that easy.

One by one, the other kids tried to make the jump. It was crazy hard.

The Gauntlet had high and low places to land. Some were very close together. Others were far apart. A few even wobbled when you landed on them.

Corrine was smart. She watched and watched, studying what the others did right and wrong.

The first kid fell right away. He landed with a thud in the sand. Two more kids tried. They got further, but both slipped off. One grabbed the sides and tried to hang on. After a few seconds, he fell anyway. More and more kids tried. Only ten made it through without falling.

Even Audrey tried. She made it almost to the end. Audrey was very good, but she didn't practice like Corrine did. On the very last jump Audrey's left foot slipped. Audrey wobbled off the platform. She threw her arms out and tried to keep her balance, but it didn't work. Audrey hit the ground hard.

She walked back with tears in her eyes.

Corrine hugged her. "Are you okay?"

"Yes," Audrey answered, quietly. "I'm okay. I didn't think I was going to win anyway. You're much better at this than I am."

"That's not true," Corrine argued.

"Yes it is, and you know it! Believe me, or you're gonna fall. You're the best jumper I've ever seen! Now go!"

Corrine turned. She was the last one.

Slowly, she walked up the stairs. Corrine climbed to the top and looked across the Gauntlet. The long line of jumping platforms looked hard. She held her breath and stepped off.

Corrine dropped to the first platform. It was very skinny and hard to land on. She wobbled a little bit but stayed on. The next platform was higher. Jumping as hard as she could, Corrine tried to land just right.

*Don't be silly!* she yelled to herself. *You've done this a thousand times!*

One platform after another flew by. Keeping her eyes on the next and the next, she jumped higher and higher. Corrine felt like a bird again.

Then, she stopped. Corrine almost lost her balance!

*Where's the next platform?!* she wondered.

Suddenly, she heard the kids clapping. Corrine was on the other side already!

*I did it!!!* she screamed inside. *How did that even happen?*

Before she could step off the stairs, Audrey sprinted over and gave her a big hug.

"You made it! I knew you would. That didn't even look hard! I'm so proud of you!"

"Thank you, Audrey!" Corrine shouted with glee. "There's still only five finalists though. They might not choose me."

"Twelve kids finished the Gauntlet. I think you were the best jumper. They would have to be crazy not to choose you!" Audrey exclaimed.

"Thanks Audrey. That means a lot."

Just as Corrine thought, the Rockets soon gathered closely. They talked while the other kids waited. After a while, the Rockets formed a line in front of the whole crowd.

"Jumpers!" Aaron announced. "You tried hard today! We had twelve finish the course. From that twelve, we normally choose only five to join us on the final jump! Twelve jumpers form a line in front!!"

Corrine did as she was told. Now there were nine Rockets standing in a row in front of the twelve contestants.

The tall Rocket, the pretty Asian girl who made the first jump, stepped up. She walked up to each of the twelve kids, leaned forward, and whispered something in their ear. She told them "yes" or "no".

Some sadly walked away. It was clear to them. They didn't make the finals. Others started jumping up and down happily. They had made it.

Slowly, the tall Rocket girl walked down to the end of the line. Four kids had been chosen. Now, there were only two left, Corrine and one other young girl.

Corrine squeezed her eyes shut. The Asian girl walked up. She whispered in the younger girl's ear.

"What is your name, contestant?"

"Samantha," the girl answered.

"Your abilities need work. Your jumping skills were flawed in many ways."

"I understand, Mistress Rocket," Samantha sighed.

"We feel you handled the Gauntlet well enough. You've made it to the finals."

A wide grin burst out on the girl's face. She clasped both hands to her chest and wriggled with joy! The girl spit out, "Thank you, Mistress Rocket! Thank you, Mistress Rocket!!!" Then Samantha ran over to join the finalists.

Corrine's heart sank. The five finalists were already chosen. She didn't make it. Her head hung low.

The tall Asian Rocket stepped over to her.

"What is your name?"

Corrine swallowed hard. "Corrine," she answered. "Can I ask you a question?"

Her request was very rude! The Asian Rocket grew stiff, but she asked, "What?!"

Corrine twirled. "I know I didn't win. That's okay. Still, I think the name "Rockets" is silly. I think you should be called the "Dolphins". They used to swim in the ocean, and they dare to dream! I have a carving of a dolphin made of apple wood, and..."

Corrine was chattering on and on.

A weird look spread across the tall girl's face. She ignored the request. Instead, she added with a frightening voice, "Your first landing was wobbly."

"I know, Mistress." Corrine's face fell. She shifted her feet around. "I was nervous."

"Stay where you are," the Asian Rocket commanded.

"Yes, Mistress." Corrine was confused. *Why isn't she telling me to leave the group?* she wondered.

The tall Asian Rocket walked over to Aaron. She said something to him. Then, she joined the others in the line. Aaron walked back up to the platform.

"Here you have them! Your five finalists are ready to compete again!"

The crowd erupted with cheering. Corrine clapped too, but she felt funny. She wasn't standing with the finalists. She wasn't back with the crowd. Corrine felt so weird standing in the middle.

"Your finalists are Derrick, Sandy, Matthew, Tony, and Samantha. Why then do we have another girl in the middle?" Aaron asked as the crowd grew quiet. "This year we were impressed! This year so many were good! They were better than good! They were great! So, this year, we are making an exception! This girl in the middle...her name is Corrine...and she was awesome too!!!"

Corrine beamed with pride. She felt like a fire burned in her belly. There were no slimy worms in her now! She was unstoppable!

"Due to her," Aaron screamed, "this year, we will have SIX finalists!!! Corrine, join us up here!!!!!"

Corrine ran to the front of the line. The six finalists stood together, strong. She was so, so happy!

And then the Gauntlet changed...

Chapter 10
Braving the Gauntlet!


Corrine gulped.

The Rockets grabbed the giant platforms and turned them. The lowest platforms got lower. The highest ones got higher. They even pushed the furthest ones further! The whole Gauntlet changed.

That wasn't all. The Rockets added cones in the middle of some of the platforms too. The finalists weren't allowed to land on those platforms!

To everyone's surprise, the Rockets turned off all the strings of electric lights. Then, they lit the Gauntlet on fire! Flames shot out from the sides. The whole clearing gleamed bright orange!

Marching up the stairs, all the contestants joined Aaron on the platform. The Gauntlet was very close.

In a moment she would begin another trial. Corrine was scared as she looked over the Gauntlet, now covered in red and orange flames.

Audrey was out there in the crowd somewhere. Corrine breathed a sigh of relief. She knew her friend was cheering for her. The crowd was awfully loud, so she pretended that all the sound came from Audrey. Everyone was clapping and screaming.

Aaron stood up next to Corrine. He was so close!

"Now," Aaron announced, "your finalists will make the jump of their life!"

He raised both arms in the air. The crowd erupted in applause.

Again the tall Asian girl made the first jump, and again she made it look so easy. The girl could jump so high. She spun in a dozen circles. Every landing was perfect! And she never looked nervous. She didn't shake or wobble once. Her jumping was so graceful.

Corrine watched. Now, the first person stepped up to the Gauntlet. It was Tony. Corrine had never met him before. He looked nice, but he was stringbean-skinny!

Tony put his hand out to time himself. His body moved in rhythm, like a song with a heavy beat. He looked like he was counting in his head. Boom.....Boom.....Boom. One....Two....Three. One..Two..Three..Then he jumped!

Tony made it to the first platform. He jumped with skill to the next and the next.

Halfway through, however, Tony made a terrible choice. He wanted to impress the crowd. There was a platform very far away with a little one in between. Tony didn't want to step on the little one! He chose to skip it, and it didn't work! The jump was way too far! Tony hit the ground hard. When he sat up, he had to spit out a whole bunch of sand!

Corrine curled her nose up. That must have tasted nasty!

The same thing happened to the other jumpers. The course was very risky. Each had hard choices to make. It was like a maze. Sometimes you ended up on a high platform. There was nowhere to go but down! They all wobbled, shook, and tumbled to the ground, one by one.

Again Corrine waited. She didn't like going first. Corrine never raised her hand to volunteer. In the end, she had no choice. Her heart beat furiously! It felt like one of the hydraulic machines was in her chest! She stepped up to the edge of the main platform.

The fire looked dreadful. The platforms looked tiny. It would be so hard to land!

She closed her eyes. Corrine took a deep breath. She pretended that she was back in the fields. She pretended that there was neither fire, crowds, Rockets, nor any other finalists. In her mind, all she could see were copper pots.

Then she opened her eyes again. Corrine was at peace. The Gauntlet didn't look as frightening anymore. It looked like a challenge, but it also looked like fun!

Corrine jumped! Her body sailed through the air. She landed on the first platform with ease. Fire burst out from under her feet. The platform was springy and bouncy. It shimmied back and forth and it even shivered, like Audrey did when she was freezing. Corrine didn't care about the platform's shimmy! She was a bird again!!!

Corrine stretched both arms out.

The crowd clapped and gasped in awe!

Corrine looked amazing as she leapt from one difficult platform to the next. She dodged cones. She ducked under bars. She even did a couple spins! In her mind, she jumped through all the copper pots.

Everyone had their mouths open.

Corrine's jumping looked almost as good as the Asian girl!

Then, Corrine got near the end. Just before the final landing, she looked for a place to leap from. She was moving so fast she couldn't see. Fire was everywhere! When she finally saw the platform, she was surprised. It was far beneath her, it was very skinny, and the whole thing was covered by a cone! It was a trick!

*What am I going to do?* Corrine panicked.

The whole crowd held their breath. Corrine was falling toward a platform that she couldn't land on! If she touched the cone, she would lose right away!

Then she saw it. There was a bar sticking out of the side.

*If I twist just right,* she thought quickly, *I might be able to grab the bar!*

Corrine turned her waist and swung her legs to the side. She wanted to be careful not to hit the cone. Then, she reached forward. The bar was coming up fast. All her fingers stretched. They went as far as they could go, and she grabbed it!!!

She couldn't believe she hung on, but then suddenly her left hand slipped off! Corrine lost control.

Everyone gasped.

Trying her best not to fall, Corrine hung on with her right hand. It was hard. She was shaking like crazy! Both of her hands were so sweaty!

Corrine tried not to wobble too much. Her body flipped over the bar three times, faster, and faster, and faster!!!

Then she let go, and shot straight up, through the flames! Corrine spun out-of-control and into a flip! She was so dizzy!

The scrapyard spun in the circular reflection of her eyes.

Corrine could barely tell where the floor, the ceiling, or even where the last platform was. At the very top she started to fall again. Corrine hoped for the best...she stuck her feet out....

...AND SHE LANDED!!!!

Chapter 11

Morticia's Evil Plan Unfolds

The whole gathering in the scrapyard was screaming, pointing, and leaping for joy!

Audrey rushed over and pulled Corrine off the ground in a giant hug! The entire crowd joined them. A hundred kids rushed upon Corrine. It was like one of the water towers had broken open, showering her with joy, but before anyone could offer congratulations, everyone stopped.

A terrible sound came from the secret tunnel. A lot of men were marching in.

The kids started scattering, yelling, and sprinting to anywhere they could flee. Even the Rockets were running around and looking worried. There was no way out.

Guards poured into the scrapyard. Each was shouting a command to halt! None of the kids listened. The men's blast sticks began hurling balls of green glowing energy. Energy splattered everywhere with that weird squishing sound.

The sticks were so powerful. Every time a blast hit someone, they were tossed high into the air! One kid even got hit in the back. He fell hard.

Corrine looked around in horror. The scrapyard had people running everywhere! How could they escape?

She studied the guards. They were wearing dark grey
armor and light grey helmets. Most were not trained well.
Many were aiming the blast sticks poorly. Sometimes they
missed. That was very dangerous. Green goo was sizzling all
over the place!

Corrine watched as some of the glowing balls flew over
their heads. The balls hit the stone ceiling. She heard
cracking and rumbling. Huge pieces of rock tumbled to the
ground with a crash!

*They're going to destroy the whole place!* she screamed
inside.

"AUDREY!" Corrine shouted while pulling Audrey behind
one of the jumping platforms. "We have to go!"

"Where?" Audrey asked.

Corrine thought about the wall of trash which encircled the
scrapyard. Maybe they could jump out. The wall was very
high. The metal garbage didn't have many things to jump
onto. It would be hard, even for Corrine. Audrey might never
make it.

As Corrine thought about it, more guards came into the
scrapyard. Less and less kids were standing. Some had
wrestled the blast sticks away and were using them
themselves. Thirty kids were fighting in the corner.

Corrine saw the Asian girl hiding behind the main platform.
They looked each other in the eyes.

The Asian girl put a finger up to her lips to say, "Be quiet!" Then she pointed up, sending Corrine a secret message.

Above the edge of the trash was a large stalactite, a giant spike coming out of the ceiling.

Suddenly, the Asian girl leapt, leaving safety behind. One of the guards spotted her.

"You there! Freeze!" he ordered.

The Asian girl ignored Morticia's guard and started running right at him. When he pushed the button on his blast stick unleashing a fiery blast at her, she suddenly slid toward the ground. She was moving so fast! As she dropped, the drippy ball of green goo went right over her! The bright light sailed above. Under it, she slid right across the scrapyard floor. Rolling to her feet, the Asian Rocket grabbed the guard. They began wrestling. Again and again she pushed the stick's button. She even tried to pull it away from him.

One ball of energy after another shot around the arena. Most shots hit the scrapyard walls. Trash broke away and fell down.

Getting the same idea, the other kids copied the Asian Rocket, grabbing a blast stick and using it to open holes in their would-be prison. Some even aimed toward the ceiling! One large piece of stone after another dropped. Giant boulders crashed into the trash wall, shredding it! Many new pathways were formed.

The guards began running for shelter. A few dropped their sticks and dove for cover away from a falling stone. The battle began turning. The kids were winning.

One of the blasts from the Asian girl was perfectly aimed too. It sailed high above and struck the stalactite right in the middle. It rumbled, crumbled, and cracked, and then it fell toward the largest wall! It was the biggest piece of rock in the whole cavern! Behind Corrine and Audrey, it drove into the ground and the wall beyond! It was so loud!!!

As the giant stalactite broke into massive boulders, Corrine realized she might be able to use them to scale the wall and escape over the other side. As soon as the dust cleared, the two girls jumped onto the settling rocks and boulders.

They ran and leapt as fast as they could. Pulling her friend along, Corrine jumped and jumped. Like rabbits, they popped up and up, again and again!

The wall was full of all sorts of trash. Pipes made for steam, green copper beams, tubs that held cream, old used machines, all became springboards to jump off so clean.

This was no contest, after all. This was for real!

Other kids were trying to jump out too and escape. One guard after another shot their sticks at them. Balls of glowing energy flew in front and behind. Corrine and Audrey ducked, dodged, and even jumped over bursts of green light.

Corrine made it to the top of the wall first. As fast as she could, Corrine looked over the other side. She froze. There was nowhere else to go from this part of the wall! Only a steep drop waited for her and Audrey. Small pieces of trash fell from her feet into the gloom below. It looked like a hole that dropped forever! Even the falling trash didn't make a sound.

*Does this part of the cavern have no floor?* Corrine panicked. *How are we going to escape?*

Jumping up was a good idea, but now they were trapped.

Corrine quickly studied the battle. She could see the whole arena, where suddenly the Asian Rocket lost her grip! The strong guard pushed her over. He knew he could aim better than anyone else. He laughed, as he turned his stick toward Audrey.

"Duck!" The Rocket girl tried shouting a warning!

But the guard's shot was too fast!

Corrine's eyes grew wide with fear.

"Audrey! Take my hand!" she yelled as the ball exploded underfoot!

Trash crumbled beneath the two girls. The copper plate they were standing on shattered.

Corrine tried jumping off the plate with Audrey in tow, but her hands were too slippery, and Corrine lost her balance! The jump didn't go right. Audrey swung around in a strange circle as she screamed! Corrine landed awkwardly on the edge of the broken copper plate. She tried again, but the wall was falling apart!

It was all happening too fast!

Her hand slipped, and Audrey tumbled back toward the
Arena. Reaching out, Corrine tried to grab her friend's hand
again, but she was an inch too far. Their fingers brushed each
other's, as they were thrown apart! Corrine spun out-of-
control, toward the open chasm.

"Corrine!" Audrey screamed!

Corrine watched in terror as Audrey bounced off a sharp
piece of pipe. Her face was covered in pain. There was
nothing Corrine could do. She was falling too fast.

"Audreeeeee...!!!"

Corrine tumbled away, into the darkness. She screamed.
Nobody heard her. Everything went dark. She fell and fell.
Her eyes could barely see.

Suddenly, a wooden board appeared. If she could land on
it, she might be able to get back and help Audrey. She tried to
jump to it, or even grab it, but she couldn't. Her body was
spinning like crazy!

Again, Corrine saw the glimmer of a copper pipe, and she
stretched, but she missed that too.

There wasn't enough time.

Abruptly, she hit the ground, but it was too steep to land
on. She felt like she was falling forever down a mountain.
Many times she rolled – head over heels. She couldn't see
anything. It was so scary!

She tumbled and tumbled down, and then she hit
something hard. Corrine saw flashes of light. Stars floated

around her head. She felt very very dizzy and a teensy bit woozy.

Then Corrine slid to a stop. Even though she couldn't see anything, she felt like the whole world was marching around her, jeering and laughing.

Corrine tried to push herself up, and she fell down. Again, she tried, and again she fell to the earth.

Lying weak on the ground, Corrine closed her eyes. She didn't know if she would ever wake up again.

Chapter 12

Peter the Super Spy


Peter took a few steps. He had to be careful. He was
sneaking through Madame Morticia's own building!

Peter was hiding behind a special set of walls. These
weren't real walls, of course. They were long thin pieces of
wood. Peter spent hours carefully painting them. He got up
very early each morning to make sure they were perfect. His
"walls" had tiny holes so he could see through them. They had
handles too. He could pick them up, take a few steps, and put
them down. Hopefully, everyone would think he was part of
the building. They took three weeks to make. When they
were done, the "walls" didn't look like wood at all. They
looked like stone.

Madame Morticia's building had real stone walls. Her walls
were very shiny. Peter wanted his fake walls to look just like
hers, and he wanted to use them at just the right time. Today,
he had his chance!

Peter watched Jasper all morning. Jasper was in the Center
pacing back and forth. He wore a long black coat with maroon
edges. It even had reddish buttons, carved out of stone! It
was very cool, but then so was Jasper. By now, Peter knew

what the man's pacing meant. Jasper was investigating something, and now he was going to see Madame Morticia.

It was time.

Peter ran home and grabbed the two pieces of wood. Carefully, he made his way back, running behind the buildings.

After sneaking in the government building – Morticia's back door – Peter slowly tip-toed down one hallway after another.

Sometimes people walked by. Each time, Peter froze. He waited behind the "walls". After they left, he looked around, and then took another step. He was very clever!

By now, Jasper was probably upstairs. Peter had to be careful, but he had to hurry too.

He started to move faster. Many people walked by. As he got closer to her office, Peter got braver and braver! Sometimes he took three or four steps. Sometimes he took ten! And sometimes he even ran down a whole hallway before another person walked by!!!

Nobody ever noticed him!

Finally, he made it to Madame Morticia's door. Morticia was in the middle of talking.

\*\*\*

"The games are against the law!" Madame Morticia yelled.

"I know. I know." Jasper's voice was both kind and serious. "We've known about them for a long time. We may not always know *where* the games are, but they're no secret. Didn't you say a long time ago the games were important? Didn't you argue that we needed to let the kids feel sneaky? You said when the kids feel sneaky, they feel happy. Why do we need to stop the games now?"

In return Morticia said, "Something has changed. The Rockets are going to be attacked. What was the other team's name, the Hurricanes?"

"Yes, they're called the Hurricanes." Jasper tried to calm her down. "This happens every year. The kids train, and they have tryouts, and they invite a new person to join them. Then they train again, very hard. Finally, they compete against each other. The winners get the right to brag for a year, and there's a trophy. I know it's dangerous, but the kids have been at peace with each other for a while. I think it's because of the games. We should let it continue. Really, it's mostly harmless," Jasper explained. He had a strong deep voice.

Morticia's building was large and white outside. Inside, it had a lot of sculptures, paintings, and plants. It looked peaceful from afar.

Today though, Morticia wasn't feeling very peaceful. She was upset, like she-just-bit-her-tongue upset! Jasper was telling her what to do. She did not like that, not at all!

Morticia stormed back and forth when they spoke. Her mood was quirky, irky, murky, and not at all smirky!

Morticia's office was very large. It had beautiful windows which overlooked the whole Center. She had tables, chairs, and wood carvings in her office. She also had a red desk and red curtains.

Sometimes she slammed both fists onto the desk. Other times she marched over to the window. When she did, she wasn't looking at anything. Morticia was too mad!

"Not this year!" she went on. "This year we're afraid they are going to fight for real. We heard they are making weapons, like the old days, swords and spears. Many of the kids are getting angry. The trophy isn't enough anymore. They say the leader of the Hurricanes, Cutter, wants to crush the Rockets for good."

"Where are you hearing all this?" Jasper wondered.

"I have my sources," Morticia answered. She wasn't going to tell him any more. Instead, she chose to talk about something else. She waited a long time and then said, "There's also a girl I want to talk to you about. Her name is Corrine."

Morticia studied Jasper. She wondered, *How would he act when I mention Corrine? Would he get all sweaty? Would he feel weird and shift around?*

Not him! Jasper didn't move an eyelash. He was very cool!

"Oh? Isn't that the girl with the disability?" he asked as if he had never met Corrine.

"Yes, the girl who forgets. There's another problem. She might be trying out for the team. She and her friend Audrey were spotted at the Column. I'm afraid she might be thinking of trying to make the jump up the Column."

Jasper frowned. "No one can make a jump like that. Besides, it's frozen outside. There's nowhere to go. All the kids know that."

"That's just the problem. Corrine forgets. She has forgotten it's frozen, and she has forgotten that she tried to make the jump already!"

"What?!" That was clearly news to Jasper.

"That's right. She tried three times before. Each time we found her on the ground below, half-dead. She fell every time."

"So what's your plan?" Jasper asked.

"I think the games need to end," Morticia said with a sly look in her eye. "They at least need to stop for a long while. Maybe the kids can sneak off and play something else. If Corrine makes the team, she will try to jump the Column again. It'll kill her. That's why I placed guards at the Column's entrance."

"Really? I didn't know all that." In truth, Jasper didn't. "Morticia, there's something I've heard about that girl."

"What?" Morticia nearly jumped out of her skin! Jasper just pretended he didn't know her, now he might be slipping! He might admit something about Corrine!

Jasper was much too cool for that! He continued, "I was wondering. I've heard she forgets a lot of important things. She forgets her home. She forgets what she did yesterday. She even forgets her friends. I think it's strange. There are some things she never forgets. She doesn't forget her job. She doesn't forget how to plant. She forgets some things and not others. Don't you think that's odd?"

Jasper was smart. His voice had power. When he spoke, others listened. His questions had layers, like the different colors of the cave walls. Most people were happy to listen to him speak.

Morticia's eyes got extra slanty. Jasper was no fool! He was trying to learn details about Corrine, and that made him a threat. Madame Morticia thought she was the one asking questions! It was the other way around! Jasper was very smart – too smart. She was going to have to watch out for him.

"I don't know," Madame Morticia answered. She wasn't going to give him anything! "It's hard to say how her disability works. All I know is that this whole jumping game is coming to a stop, or else!"

Morticia was the head of the Province. She was no fool, and she didn't need his help to end the games. She had the power already, and now she knew there was no getting him on her side. Morticia moved to her next plan.

Morticia could see the wheels turning in his head. He was figuring out her plan right in front of her. She could sense that he was picturing the guards lining up. He was imagining their armor, their helmets, and their blast sticks!

The games were today. Jasper was the only one with a strong voice. If he asked the guards to stop, they would listen. Morticia needed Jasper out of the way.

"What have you done, Morticia?" Jasper took a step forward. His voice growled.

"I did what had to be done!" she answered with an angry look in her eyes. She even gave him a crooked smile, knowing she already snapped Jasper's thoughts right out of his head.

"You are wrong, Morticia! Are you going to risk their lives? They're kids! You are using power in the worst way! Yes, they are breaking the rules, but the rules you are breaking are far more terrible!!!"

"How dare you?! How can you say such things to me?! You are removed from this office!" Morticia yelled back. "I am the power here! I am the only power!"

Jasper spun around. He marched toward the doors, opening them widely.

Before he left, Jasper turned toward her again. His long black coat with the maroon edges spun around him. He looked strong and confident. He stuck his chin out and said with a loud and clear voice, "The other Overseers will agree with me!  Your rule here has come to its end!!!"

Then Jasper slammed the doors shut!

Jasper was very cool.

Chapter 13

The Mystery of Corrine

Jasper took in a heavy breath. He looked at the doors of
Madame Morticia's office. They were closed for good.
Nothing between them would ever be the same. Madame
Morticia needed to be stopped.

Fifty, a hundred, or even more of Morticia's guards were
going to attack the Rockets! He had to get to the tryouts fast.
Morticia was going to force the games to end today, but
something much worse was happening.

Morticia was becoming a person who ruled by fear! That
would be terrible! If she remained as their leader, it would be
very bad for the Province.

He looked around the foyer and the long hallway.
Something seemed different.

Jasper started to hurry off. He was thinking about too
much right now. This was not the time to worry about minor
things.

Still, the tiny voice that tells you something is wrong
nagged him. It was a little creepy. He walked down the whole
hallway with the feeling. He walked to the stairwell with it.
He even stepped down the first steps, and then he spun
around.

Somebody was watching him. He knew it. All the hairs on his neck were standing up.

Jasper took a slow step back into the foyer. He studied it. Nothing moved. Then he closed his eyes.

Jasper was indeed smart!

In his mind, he called up a picture of the foyer. When he opened his eyes again, something was different. In the corner, there was a set of walls which weren't there before. Only one person in a hundred thousand million would ever have noticed!

Jasper walked right up to the corner and leaned in close. The walls were fake! Someone painted these walls to look like real walls. He grabbed the tops and tore them away. Peter was hiding right behind it!

Quickly, Peter squirted oil into Jasper's face. Jasper was too fast. Jasper's head looked like an apple branch when someone suddenly jumps off, snapping to the side.

Jasper was so quick. In a flash, Jasper dodged the oil and grabbed Peter.

Peter yelped, and Jasper threw a fast hand over Peter's mouth. In turn, Peter clasped something copper onto Jasper's wrist. It had a lot of wires and electricity began to shoot out! Jasper winced in pain, but he didn't let go.

"Hush, Peter!" Jasper grunted. "We need to get out of here! This building isn't safe anymore!"

\*\*\*

As they crossed the Mecca, Peter studied Jasper. Peter watched the man's every move, wondering if Jasper would make a better ruler for the Province.

At first, Jasper had a tight grip on Peter's arm. Jasper guided Peter away from Madame Morticia's office.

Jasper had a lot of respect. People nodded and smiled in the hallway. Peter began to relax. He thought he was in deep trouble when Jasper grabbed him, but not anymore. For some reason, Jasper was protecting him. After a while, Jasper even let Peter walk on his own.

They left Morticia's building and crossed the Center. Everyone had respect for Jasper. He smiled and told everyone they were doing a good job. No one knew what had just happened. It didn't matter to them either way. He smiled and shook their hands. He patted them on the back in a kind way.

Peter realized something. Good people don't care what title you have. They don't care about your badge. They don't care which office is yours. They only care about the way you treat them. If you treat them nice, they will always be loyal.

Jasper was well-liked. He was so cool!

Then, a few guards in the Center took notice and watched Jasper and Peter. More than one started speaking on their headsets. Madame Morticia must have been getting the word out! She thought Jasper was a traitor!

Abruptly, each of the guards moved quickly toward Jasper and Peter! Jasper grabbed Peter's arm again. They began running together.

Jasper and Peter had to hurry. They dodged around crowds of people. Maybe if Jasper and Peter got there quick enough, they could stop it.

As they ran, Peter worried. Madame Morticia was very powerful. He didn't know if Jasper was strong enough to stop her. That would require a whole lot of cool!!!

The guards chased them out of the Center and into the suburbs of the Province.

Jasper hurried. He ducked around people carrying buckets, and carpenters carrying wooden beams. Jasper and Peter flew like the wind. Jasper's black coat with the maroon edges flowed like an ancient bird of prey, like a hawk! He looked dark and spooky. Peter grinned! Maybe Jasper had just enough cool!!

They weaved between hundreds of people. Many jumped out of the way. Jasper used all sorts of ways to hide, under laundry, behind barrels, and even inside doorways.

After running for a while, Jasper pulled Peter into a dark corner between two houses.

"I talked to Corrine last week, in the Center," he said hurriedly, "At first she drove me nuts, but she caught my eye because she refused to look sad. Corrine walked around like she saw a sunny day, not the cavern ceiling. I had to talk to

her. She told me that we were planting all wrong. I asked her
to write it down. The next day she gave me pages upon pages!
Peter, Corrine wrote over a hundred pages, in one night!"

Jasper dug some of the pages out of his black coat. After he
did, he suddenly pulled Peter deeper into the shadows.
Outside, two guards ran by.

Jasper breathed a sigh of relief and continued, "Look at
what she wrote."

Peter started to read the papers. The first page was a list of
directions for the Province. It was all Corrine needed to
replant the fields.

*What were all the other papers for?* Peter wondered. He
continued flipping through page after page.

The directions went on and on! There were lists for
gardens, landscapes, and even whole countries! Corrine had
drawn lots of pictures. There were lists of trees, like the
mighty redwood, the sea grape tree of the Islands, and even
the beautiful shea tree of Nigeria. There were lists of flowers,
bushes, types of grass and mosses, vegetables, and vines too!
There were drawings of plants Peter had never seen!

Some of the books Peter had had pictures of these plants.
Corrine didn't read like Peter did. He knew that. How then
did she know all this?

Peter looked back at Jasper, confused.

"I know," Jasper pulled the words right out of Peter's
mouth. "There's something special about her. She is no

ordinary twelve year old. These papers are directions to replant the whole earth! Who is she? There is a mystery surrounding her, and I need you to solve it."

"Why me?" Peter asked.

"Because, at the end of today, you won't see me for a while. Madame Morticia has a lot of power. I'm going to the games to save the kids, and Morticia will probably arrest me. For now, we need to make it to the scrapyard. Can you help me find the entrance to the games?"

"I sure can!" Peter shouted with glee!

The ten guards looking for them were gone now. Peter thought that was strange. Normally, the Center had more soldiers around. Today, the Center was empty of guards, as only ten men were in the hot pursuit.

That's when Peter knew Jasper was right. The rest of Morticia's soldiers were sure to be at the games! Corrine and Audrey were in trouble!

Pulling a special set of goggles over his head, Peter studied the ground. He could see the heat from his own footprints which glowed bright red.

Carefully, Jasper and Peter snuck into the Main Street. The ground was different here.

Many footprints came this way. Peter found what he was looking for, a hundred sets of footprints all marching the same way! It was an army!

Peter followed the footprints for a long time. Finally, the red footprints led to a secret place at the edge of the Province. It was the scrapyard! As they got close, Peter and Jasper could hear loud booms from blast sticks! Peter ran even faster.

Then, Jasper stepped up to the edge of the scrapyard. Several kids were lying on the ground. These kids were supposed to keep an eye on the secret entrance. None of them were awake. Each had green goo energy dripping off their clothes. The guards had already been here!

Peter followed the red footprints through the trash. Jasper stayed close. They followed a narrow path that zigged to the right and zagged to the left. It was like a snake!

Finally, Jasper and Peter walked into a large open clearing. Guards were all over the place, and green goo was everywhere! A few kids were trapped in the middle. The guards had made them all sit together in a circle. Some were crying.

Peter dashed toward the group of kids. Nobody stopped him as he wasn't trying to escape. He searched and searched.

Peter started to worry. He couldn't see either Corrine or Audrey. Then he heard his name. Audrey was weakly waving from the other side of the clearing. Two guards were next to her. She looked really hurt.

"Are you okay?" Peter ran up.

"No." Audrey kept looking away. She was wiping tears off her cheeks.

"What happened?!"

"I have a few cuts and some bruises, but I'm okay. We fell off the wall. I bounced a few times. The Asian Rocket girl caught me before I hit the ground. Peter, I think Corrine is dead. She fell off the other side. The guards called it "the deep chasm". They say it has no bottom!"

Jasper walked up. He never had to ask the guards. They had too much respect for him. He heard what Audrey just said about Corrine. Jasper never looked so sad! Peter thought the man was going to cry, but his face was quickly changing. He got angrier and angrier!

"What's wrong with you?!" he screamed at the guards. "What's wrong with all of you?! You could have gotten them all killed! They're a bunch of kids. Were you trying to cause a cave-in? You could all be dead! Who ordered this?!!!"

Peter could tell that Jasper knew the answer already. He was making a point. He wanted everyone else to know. Several guards were ashamed. They took their helmets off and hung their heads low. Most of them weren't much older than the Rockets. Jasper asked them some pretty hard questions. They kept looking at him and shifting their feet.

"Let them go!" Jasper started ordering the guards around. "Let them go. They haven't really done anything wrong."

"They attacked my men," an important guard said stiffly. His dark grey armor had yellow lines on the sides. He was a captain.

"Were they causing trouble, or were they trying to have fun? For goodness sake, it's boring down here in the caves. You know that. They need to do something sometime! They weren't attacking you. They were defending themselves." Jasper tried to reason.

Several of the kids rose. Many of the guards were looking back and forth. They looked like they didn't know what to do. Jasper *was* an Overseer. Each looked at the captain.

"Let them go. It's okay," the captain said. "We only came for the Rockets."

The kids began slowly leaving the cavern. Some of them left through the clearing's entrance back to the edge of the scrapyard. Others knew different routes. They climbed through the new holes in the walls. A lot walked on a bad foot, and a few nursed a sore elbow. There were so many who got hurt. Slowly, everyone disappeared.

After a few minutes all the kids were gone, except for the Rockets, Peter and Audrey. The Rockets were still under arrest. As the guards walked them out, the Asian Rocket passed by Audrey.

"My name's Kojika," she winked and pointed at Audrey. "Don't worry about us now. You were good, kid. You have potential. Keep working on it!"

Chapter 14

Escaping Morticia's Claws


Peter and Audrey were left behind with Jasper.

Suddenly, the guards started looking toward the clearing's entrance.

Peter froze! Ten more guards – the same ones who were chasing Jasper earlier – marched in. Behind them walked several Overseers and then Madame Morticia! A deep scowl was on her face! She looked ready to argue!

Alongside her was the Province General, Rodney! Some said he used to talk. Now, he never said a word. No one was alive who remembered him speaking. Instead, he used hand signals. They called it sign-language. It was said, a long time ago, he was a soldier, a real soldier. Now, he had a lot of grey in his hair, but he was still a good General. Rodney was very tall, very wide, and he had a lot of muscles! It was frightening to even look at him! Also he had even darker skin than Jasper, like Corrine.

Jasper turned to Peter and Audrey, and said, "Quick! When they aren't looking, escape through one of the holes. I have a mystery for you to solve. Go to the Eastern Province. Find an old woman named Ethel. There's a special computer in the Mecca, with a lot of information stored on it. I'm not sure why. I found Ethyl's name in the archives. She must know something."

Then Jasper jumped up. He was so strong. Instead of hiding, he stormed right up to Madame Morticia without any fear!

"Look at what you've done!" he accused her. "Did you see the injuries? Did you see the kids limping and coughing? What about Corrine?! She fell into the deep chasm over the wall! Is that what you wanted, to kill her? Is this to be the future? Are you going to rule only with weapons? Isn't one of our most sacred rules to bring no guns? When did you start crafting them, after all this time?!!"

"That's enough out of you!" Morticia spit the words out. "You're under arrest for crimes against the Province."

Then, Madame Morticia turned her evil glare. Her black and white bun whipped around. She glared at the other Overseers. Rodney waited next to her.

The air was very tense.

Jasper held his head up high no matter what. Jasper was very tall and strong too. Next to Rodney though he looked half the size! Still, he didn't look the least bit afraid.

*He was the coolest of the cool!!!* Peter thought.

Rodney looked back and forth. Madame Morticia *was* the head of the Province. They all agreed to follow her rules, and so Rodney raised his huge arm and gave the sign to "Come here". The ten guards who came in with him made a circle around Jasper.

Under close watch, they made Jasper leave. Jasper would have to answer for the things he said, and for letting some of the kids go. They would probably take him to the courthouse. Everyone would call him a traitor.

Madame Morticia swiveled her head back to Peter and Audrey. Her eyes got more slantier than ever!

Audrey panicked! They forgot to try and escape!

"Let's go!" Peter shouted. Peter grabbed Audrey's arm and dove into the closest opening in the trash.

"Stop them!" Morticia ordered.

Several poorly trained guards pointed their blast sticks. They were too late. Peter and Audrey leapt through the hole just in time! Green goo squirted all over the place! The energy exploded with so much power! Trash fell everywhere, even over the hole. It would be hard for the guards to follow now.

"What are you waiting for! Go after them!" Peter heard Morticia scream.

Quickly, the guards ran up to the wall and started pulling the trash away. Peter and Audrey ran and ran. Audrey had a sore arm and a bruised knee, but she was okay. They dodged around one corner after another.

The guards followed for a long while. There were so many of them! Sometimes green energy burst just over the twosome's heads!

The scrapyard was a giant maze. It was hard to run through, but that was good, because the confusing maze gave the guards a run for their money.

Every tiptoe Peter and Audrey took made a lot of noise. The ground was icky, prickey, sticky, and very very tricky! It made sneaking around hard!

The two kids jumped inside rubber tires, and across the hoods of very old trucks. They hid under heaps of wood with bendy copper nails. They even climbed on top of old machine parts and held their breath. Guards ran everywhere.

Peter used every trick he had. He shot oil at them. That made the guards slip and slide all over the place! He used sparkle flares too. Brilliant spinning light blinded two of the guards. He even threw out two heavy copper balls attached by wires. Those tangled around the guard's feet. Ten men ended up in a giant pile after that!

Peter and Audrey giggled as they ran. This whole adventure was way too much fun!

At the far end of the scrapyard, they found some small homes. They had to hide behind them for a long time to catch their breath. Finally, after what felt like forever, Peter realized that they had gotten away! No guards were chasing them now!

Peter looked around. Peter had never seen this part of the Province before. The people here were very poor. Audrey had never seen poverty like this. Hundreds of tiny houses were clustered together. Black soot covered the eyes of the people. They stared at the two kids with a hollow look. It was so creepy!

"Where are we?" Audrey whispered. She grabbed Peter's arm and hid behind him.

"We're at the edge of the Eastern Province."

"The Eastern Province?!" Audrey yelled. "How did we get here?"

"The scrapyard must connect the Southern and Eastern Provinces," Peter answered. "Look here."

Peter picked up an old discarded pipe. He drew a large plus sign in the dirt. He pointed to the middle and explained, "This is the Center, the Mecca. Up top is the Northern Province, called the Fields, which you know. That's where most of the orphans and farmers live. To the left is the Western Province, or Machine Town. My orphanage is right here, between the upper hydraulic machines." Peter tapped his pipe onto the ground, making a dot for his house. "Down the bottom is the Southern Province, home of the Farmers and Makers. They craft wood and copper and they have all the animals. Finally, to the right is Mining Town."

Peter then drew four more lines. Each line connected the edges. Now the plus sign looked like a kite! He pointed to the

top right and said, "This area is where the Column is." Then
he added, "The top left are the caves we sneak through to play
together. It's also where the Hurricanes practice. The bottom
left is where I followed Jasper to the hidden room. It's also
where the Falls are and Daggers Hollow. Finally, on the
bottom right is the scrapyard."

"It's so pretty!" Audrey exclaimed, "It looks like a beautiful
diamond!"

Peter smiled. He liked how happy she always was. Again
he pointed at the map. "You and Corrine came down from the
top this morning. You walked past the Mecca and down into
the Southern Province. Then you went over to the right side
of my drawing, through the scrapyard, and now we are over
here." Peter finally drew an "X" on the far right. They were
clearly in the Eastern Province.

"Wow," Audrey whispered. "I've never seen it drawn out
like that. You're so good at these types of things!" She looked
around. "I've never been to Mining Town before. It looks so
sad and dreary!"

"They don't have as much to trade. They mine copper, a
few other metals, and mostly sooty coal for the hydraulic
machines. The other corners of the Province have more
money."

Audrey continued to walk behind Peter. Her eyes were
wide with fright! She stared back at all the people who
mumbled to each other.

The Eastern Province didn't get visitors very often!

Everything Peter touched was covered by a thin layer of black dust. There weren't many lights, and the ones the homes did have were orange and very dim.

The people coughed a lot too. They coughed inside the homes and outside. The sounds were everywhere. When anyone coughed, dust floated up around them into a dark cloud. It was hard to breathe.

"Why did Jasper want us to come here?" Audrey asked. "We could have been looking for Corrine."

"The guards will look for Corrine. Jasper knew that. Madame Morticia will look very bad if one of her guards killed an orphan. Jasper's been searching all over the Province, but he's never come here. He wants us to help solve a mystery for him."

"What mystery? That's exciting!" Audrey jumped for joy.

From that point on, Peter could tell she stopped being afraid.

It was time to find Ethel! Ethel was old. She must have known what the Province was like a long time ago. Jasper was onto something, and they were gonna learn it from her!

Chapter 15

A Rebellion in the Underground Province


Jasper clenched his teeth.

The guards marched him and their other prisoners all the way back to the Mecca. People from all over the Province stared. Their mouths hung way open! So many had been arrested. The guards forced all the Rockets to walk in a long line.

"Keep moving!" they ordered. "Don't slow down!"

When they reached the Center, they turned toward Rodney's building. The guards met there everyday. Usually, they went upstairs to train, but not today. After going in the front door, the guards made Jasper and the Rockets file downstairs.

At the bottom was a dark dungeon. Down the middle of the dungeon was a long hallway and on both sides were rows of cells. The walls, the ceiling, and the floor were made of big stone boulders, and the prison bars were made of heavy copper. It was more than a dark dungeon! It was a super duper dark dungeon!! No one was going to escape from here.

Rodney stepped down the stairs. His heavy footsteps made a deep noise. They were slow and frightening. Thump-Thump. Thump-Thump. He wore a long black cape. It swayed with every step. His mood was dark. Rodney pointed a thick finger at clusters of the kids. Then he pointed at a cell. It was like he was saying, "You, you, you, and you! In!!"

Rodney broke them into smaller groups.

Jasper was last. He was the only one who stood up to Rodney. At the very end of the hall, Jasper refused to move. The kids all took in a fearful breath. Rodney was much taller, and twice as wide as Jasper.

Rodney's mouth growled. Slowly, he signed a single word: "Traitor".

For a whole minute the air was tense. No one moved.

"Am I?" Jasper questioned without sounding disrespectful. "Am I the traitor? The people aren't happy. We have survived for a while. Maybe you cannot speak, but you are not deaf. The air is changing. You see the dust. You hear the coughing. You hear the complaints. You hear the hydraulics grinding down. Everything here is dying. Poverty is growing, and you know it!"

Rodney looked stunned. He stood there for a long time. When he did answer, it was short and confusing.

In sign language, there is no word for "is". He signed simply: "Follow orders. Good for Province."

Jasper responded quickly, "Rodney, whose orders are YOU following? Those guards with the grey helmets weren't your men, were they? Why is Morticia training a new army? We have had peace for decades. You have only needed, what, a few dozen guards to watch the Center and the Column? These new ones are workers, aren't they? Morticia pulled miners off the copper lines. They didn't even know how to aim their blast sticks. It almost caused a cave-in! They attacked defenseless kids, and you want to follow her orders?"

Jasper's words stung like a pair of whacked shins. Rodney's head hung low. He pointed to the cell again.

This time, Jasper walked in, willingly. He knew he was about to face a trial. This was going to be huge. The whole future of the Province was at stake.

"Let them go, Rodney. This is wrong, and you know it!" Jasper pulled his own cell door shut. "Children are like a spring between your fingers. Hold them too loose, and they'll fall so often they'll never grow right. Hold them too tight, and when the time is right, they'll explode! Do the right thing, Rodney."

Rodney took a minute to look up and down the hallway.

The Rockets took in a worried breath. Each of them stepped up to the bars. They looked back at the Province General.

Rodney turned back to Jasper. No one knew what he would do next.

***

"You did what?!" Morticia roared. She was like a volcano ready to explode!

"I let them go," Rodney signed. "Jasper not right about you. Morticia, you good. Jasper right about the kids. They harmless."

"The Province is getting too old," Morticia answered. "Everyone is starting to question me. There's trouble in the air. Something needs to be done. Are you with me?"

Rodney paused and signed, "Yes."

Morticia blinked. She was stunned. He actually paused before answering!

Morticia flopped into her chair. She rubbed her forehead and thought.

Jasper was speaking lies. Corrine was gone for good. The Rockets were doing whatever they wanted. Other kids would follow, and soon no one would obey Rodney. He was getting soft. Jasper was getting to him. The young Overseer was sneaking around the Province asking questions. She told the other Overseers not to trust Jasper. They were listening to her, for now. Morticia was still worried. Jasper's voice was getting stronger. She couldn't allow someone to speak against her like that.

Suddenly, a sneaky evil thought occurred to her, and she needed to get all the Overseers and the Leaders to join together in the Mecca. The Rockets and Hurricanes would soon compete at Daggers Hollow. It wouldn't be too difficult to eliminate the entire Province, almost everybody, and start over. Maybe if a terrible accident happened...

"Rodney," she jumped up and asked, "Can you find the girl who runs the fields for me? What was her name?"

"L-I-N-D-A," he spelled out the letters. The teenager's name didn't come up that often.

"That's right, Linda. Get her for me. Also, we need to plan the trial. It can't be small and private. Jasper's trial needs to be in the open, in the courthouse. We'll invite everybody to the Mecca. They'll see for themselves the price of treachery!"

When she looked up, Rodney signed again, "What about other girl?"

"Corrine? My guards found the poor girl," Morticia answered, trying to sound sad. "I'm sorry, Rodney. It's Jasper's fault. He was supposed to stop the games. None of the kids should have been there to begin with! Corrine didn't make it out alive."

## Chapter 16
### Discovering a Clue – An Old Photograph


Audrey watched Peter, and she appreciated his bravery.
Peter had a lot of courage. He banged on so many doors.
Sometimes the people inside were frightening. Many were big
men with lots of muscles. When they opened the door they
seemed angry. Peter didn't care. He spoke nicely. Soon even
the biggest, scariest men were laughing!

Audrey was surprised. She learned that when we are polite,
other people like us more. When Peter respected them, they
respected him!

Peter asked each person if they knew where Ethel lived.
Most didn't.

The Eastern Province was very large. They went through
one neighborhood after another. All the homes were falling
apart. Audrey didn't think anyone could be happy there.

Finally, at the very end, one woman had heard of Ethyl.
The woman pointed across the neighborhood. Then later,
another man said Ethyl lived at the end of a long row of
homes!

When they got to Ethel's house, Audrey thought it was the
smallest of all the homes, buried in a tiny corner. Audrey was

surprised she could see the house at all. The street was so dark.

This time it was Audrey who knocked on the door.

A grouchy looking elderly lady came to the door. She was the oldest person Audrey had ever seen! The elderly woman had an old worn cane. It was made of apple wood. She wore a yellow flowery dress. Her silvery hair was tied in a long frizzy braid. She wore a thick pair of spectacles too, and her eyes looked huge, like the eyes of a giant fish. The elderly woman must have been blind without the glasses.

"Yes? Can I help you?" The woman stared at the two kids.

"Hello ma'am. May we ask you a few questions?" Audrey used her nicest tone.

"Umm...no..." the woman mumbled. "You're not from around here, are you?"

She sounded afraid. Audrey began to think the woman didn't get a lot of visitors.

"No," Peter answered politely, "This is Audrey. She's from the Northern Province. I'm Peter. I'm from Machine Town. We have some questions about the Province."

"You have questions about the Province? That's strange." The woman rubbed her chin. "No, I'm too old to think about things like that."

Ethel grabbed the door handle.

"Jasper sent us here!" Peter exclaimed.

"Poppycock! I don't know any Jasper, and I don't have time for this nonsense!!" Ethel grumbled and began shutting the door.

"It's about Corrine!" Audrey blurted out.

"Corrine?!" Ethel's huge eyes opened even wider! Swinging the door open again in a flurry, Ethel looked excited. "Where is she? Is she here? Is she with you?"

"No," Audrey said sadly. Soft tears were suddenly dripping down her face. "She fell into a deep chasm. I don't think we are ever going to see her again."

Peter looked down at his shoes. He began playing with small rocks at his feet for no reason. He appeared sad too.

"Did you know her?" Audrey continued.

"Yes. I knew Corrine." Ethel leaned forward. Pushing her thick glasses up, she looked back and forth suspiciously. Suddenly, she looked very nervous. Then she asked, "Does Morticia know you're here?"

Peter looked like he was ready to jump out of his shoes, he was so surprised, and Audrey giggled for a second. How would an old woman, living very far away, know Corrine? This was getting weird!

"Well, come in, come in..." she repeated, "...before someone sees."

Ushering them inside, Ethel pointed at a couple chairs. They looked rickety and almost ready to break. Audrey and

Peter both sat down. The chairs creaked, but they held for
now.

Ethel's house was small. She had an easy chair of her own,
a lamp, and a bunch of dusty books. Her bed was made of a
few planks of wood and a chicken feather mattress. Ethel had
heaps of blankets for the cold months, and more heaps for the
very cold months. Her house was very simple. Even her
"tables" were made of piles of suitcases. Everything was
ancient!

"I've lived down here for many years. You get used to a
simple way of life," Ethel explained. "I've kept my mouth shut
for a very long time. Madame Morticia is terribly powerful.
Let me tell the two of you a story. A long time ago, when I was
a little girl, we ran from the ice storms."

Audrey looked at Peter in shock! Audrey's eyebrows
jumped to the top of her forehead, and so did Peter's. She
didn't know anyone who remembered the ice storms.

"We were lucky to find the caves," Ethel went on. "In the
rush to escape, I lost my glasses. I was blind for many years.
We would have met the same fate as the rest of earth – frozen!
We lived down here for a while. Life got hard. Water was
scarce. That was before we found the Falls, waterfalls they
were called, where the strong men built pipes for fresh water.
Then the Province found metals for the hydraulic machines
and coal. I remember my parents getting upset. They argued
a lot. The adults always said they needed to go back up. I

remember the adults hugging and crying together, before different groups left. They climbed into the Lift, and up they went, out of the Province. No one ever came back. My parents left too. They didn't come back either.

"Then many years went by. There were so few adults around. I grew up and became one of them. I was about thirty years old. They called me "Blind Ethel". We had what we needed to survive. The Province was growing. The mines were getting deeper. The animals were even thriving, and a restless wind blew through the Province.

"An old scientist named Franklin said it was time to go. Mr. Franklin was very nice. He spent many long days in a lab he built. Mr. Franklin was the smartest person I ever met. He said the ice was melting. Mr. Franklin said he could fix it. There was an engine left behind in the snow that could warm the earth back up. He called it the Earth Engine. He brought out his little girl and said she was going to help everybody. She was going to save the earth! I can't be sure, but I think the older people had seen her before. People were whispering bad things about the little girl. They didn't trust her. Everyone loved Mr. Franklin though. They did trust him. So, they formed a group to climb out again. Of course, I couldn't go because I would slow them down. They were all excited. But Mr. Franklin was wrong. Most didn't come home.

"Here, let me show you a picture..."

Ethel stopped talking and started digging next to her bed. From under the blankets she pulled out a brown leather box. There were a lot of little trinkets inside. Some were rings, and others were tiny wood carvings. Finally, there was a set of worn photographs. Ethel pulled one out.

She clutched the photo close and explained, "This is a picture of the last caravan. It's forty years old. A caravan is a group of adventurers! These people certainly were. Mr. Franklin was leading the group. Madame Morticia's parents went too. So did Maureen's parents. There were other couples too. There's a couple on the left who had a son named Sampson, and another man with two boys named Robert and Michael. These were the last of the adults. They all left to save the earth, and here on the far right was Mr. Franklin's daughter."

Ethel turned the picture around. The picture was dull and faded. The corners were brown and crumbly. Peter and Audrey leaned close. It had all the people Ethel told them about. There was a whole line of adults with heavy clothes and climbing gear. The tallest one must have been the old scientist, Mr. Franklin. Lastly, on the far right, the last person in line, and standing at the very edge of the picture, was Corrine.

Audrey gasped.

"What?!" Peter shouted, "This picture is from forty years ago. Corrine is only twelve."

"I know. But it's dangerous to ask anything here –
especially any questions about Corrine. Madame Morticia
won't stand for it. There is something special about Corrine.
Mr. Franklin has white skin, as you can see. He said Corrine
was his daughter, but clearly her skin is dark. No one
questioned him, of course. Many people back then adopted
children. Corrine went with him and the caravan. They tried
climbing over a set of mountains many miles away. They fell
and got trapped."

"Corrine's dream!" Audrey exclaimed.

Peter nodded.

Ethel continued, "Mr. Franklin didn't come home.
Madame Morticia's parents both died as did most of the
others. As time went on, Morticia got more and more furious.
She suffered terrible grief, but it drove her mad. Her guards
tore the Lift down. They blocked off the Column. Everyone
understood. Her parents just died, and the ice storms were
dangerous. Aside from me, she was one of the oldest Province
members. The Province made her the leader.

"Maureen's parents survived also and a few other adults.
When they came home they were grateful to Corrine.
Everyone said she saved them. I don't know how. They were
so happy to be alive. Corrine was never the same. She didn't
play like the other little girls. She didn't talk. Corrine sat
around the Mecca and stared off at nothing. She wandered for
a long time in the caves. It was like she was trying to

remember something. Most people forgot about her. It was strange. She spent years in one part of the Province, and years in another. I think I was the only person who noticed Corrine wasn't growing older. I spoke to an Overseer about it. That was a mistake.

"Madame Morticia punished me. They moved me all the way over here. Being blind, I couldn't go far. I don't think Morticia even knows I'm still alive. After the accident in the snow, she wasn't happy at all. It wasn't Corrine's fault that Morticia's parents died, but Morticia blamed the poor child anyway. The Madame moved Corrine from place to place. She worked in the infirmary for a while, then down with the animals, and then finally in the fields.

"It's funny that you two came here. My neighbors helped me recently, just about two years ago. I went to the Mecca to get a new pair of glasses and to sell some carvings. Mistress Maureen was always nice to me. Sometimes, she would buy my carvings. A long time had passed since I traveled to the Mecca. The Center had grown so much. It used to be nothing but wooden shacks. Now there were whole buildings! I bought a small knife and a nice piece of wood, and I started to carve a dolphin. Later I found Corrine on the road that leads to the fields. She didn't remember me, but I remembered her, so I gave her the carving. The dolphin reminded me of her. That's a type of animal that used to jump out of the oceans. Corrine smiled at me. She was sitting alone and muttering to

herself, like she usually did. Everyone treated her weird.
After I gave her the dolphin, she got up and started talking to
the other kids in the field. Somehow I feel like I made a
difference."

"You certainly did!" Audrey shrieked with glee. "That was
the day Corrine and I met! She had the dolphin in her hand!!!
That's a special dolphin to us both." Audrey bounced over to
Ethel and gave her a giant hug! "You did make a difference!
We are best friends now, and it's because of you, Ethel! Thank
you so much!!!"

Ethel grinned from ear to ear. Audrey knew she made
Ethyl feel so special!

"Mark my words, honey," Ethel said. "You two have more
adventure waiting for you. If I'm right, I don't think Corrine
was the type to give up so easily. For goodness sake, she fell
off a mountain and lived to tell the tale!"

Audrey jumped. "Oh my goodness, Peter! I just realized!
Corrine's dreams were never dreams! Corrine used to work
with animals! She even worked in the infirmary! They're not
dreams; they're memories! Corrine was remembering things!"

"Then Ethel is right!" Peter announced. "Corrine herself
was Jasper's mystery. He knew something was different about
her! Why doesn't she get older? Where did she come from?
How did she save Maureen's parents and the others? And
how is she going to save the earth? We're gonna solve Jasper's
mystery! There are secrets on that computer in the Center,

but we have to go somewhere else first. We're going to go figure out who Corrine is, and I know where the answers begin! We have to go back to the hidden room!"

## Chapter 17

### Tip-toeing through the Eerie Southern Province

It was impossible for Peter and Audrey to solve the mystery quickly. Peter told her it was better to lay low for a while, and Audrey decided to listen.

The Center was full of Morticia's new guards and every pathway, tunnel, and roadway was being monitored. The guards were busy building strange grey boxes full of wires and things too. Everyone said it had something to do with the trial, but Peter told Audrey that he didn't think so. Either way, it wasn't wise to sneak down to the hidden room at the edge of Machine Town.

No one got a good look at Peter and Audrey anyway when the soldiers chased them through the scrapyard. Morticia didn't know who they were either, which was good.

For a while, the twosome could hide just by being normal. So Peter went back to the hydraulic machines, and Audrey went back to the fields for a few days.

Audrey spent the whole week uprooting. The Pickers followed all of Corrine's ideas. It was hard work. They had to be careful not to lose good soil. When everything was done, Audrey stepped back.

Before, the Fields were clustered and confusing. Now, they looked neat and orderly!

Audrey grinned! The Fields looked amazing!! Corrine's ideas *were* for the best!!!

During that week, rumors spread around. Everyone thought Corrine had died. Some of the Pickers said the Rockets got caught in the cave-in too. Audrey knew that wasn't true, but she didn't say anything. She wanted to keep quiet. Others said the Rockets were seen being marched into the dungeon, and that they would be in prison forever.

Later, Audrey heard Linda whispering with some of the older kids. Linda said she talked to Aaron himself, and he said that General Rodney let them go.

Linda warned Aaron that the Hurricanes were planning something big. They wanted revenge. Linda said Aaron got really angry and was going to plan something himself. Audrey didn't know what to believe.

Peter visited Audrey a couple times, and he was itching to go back to the hidden room. For now, going through the Center was too dangerous. Morticia's guards were still sure to be everywhere. Maybe they were looking for two kids, even now!

Then Peter and Audrey got the break they needed.

A big invitation was carried to the four corners of the Province. In two days all Lead Operators were supposed to come to the Center. Linda was a Lead Planter. That meant she was invited to come. The other Leaders were going too, the rest of the Lead Planters, the Lead Machinists, the Lead Miners...the list went on and on!

There was going to be a big announcement! The Mecca was sure to be packed. Peter and Audrey could slip through a crowd like that easily!

Two days later, it happened just like Audrey hoped. Audrey had never seen so many people in one place!

A couple thousand people gathered in the Center. The two friends easily darted around one person after another. They snuck left. They ducked right. They wormed through holes in the crowds, and they even scooted under wooden beams and buckets! Carefully, they managed to get through the whole Mecca!

Peter and Audrey crossed from the Northern part down to the entrance of the Southern Province.

From there it was eerie. Most of the streets were empty. Something was wrong. Homes sat quiet. Even the animals were silent. The cows barely moo'd. The chickens didn't cluck. Even the pigs didn't snort! Something strange was going on.

Also, there were footprints in the dirt, soldier's footprints. The tracks were everywhere, and they were all heading to the hidden room. Morticia was definitely up to something suspicious.

Peter and Audrey ducked behind one of the houses, and Audrey watched Peter eye the ground.

"Morticia knows about the hidden room, and it's sure to be protected. We should be careful," he said smartly. "Also, Morticia is up to something. She could have had Jasper's trial in private. The big announcement was meant to distract everybody. There are way more people there than just Leaders. Everyone wants to know what will happen to Jasper. Morticia knew that would happen. Her guards are all waiting there too! We have to be careful. Walk behind me."

Audrey did as she was told, after all, she knew when to trust Peter.

They walked past one empty street after another. The Southern Province was so quiet. Dust blew around Audrey's feet as she took each step.

Carefully, they followed the footprints. Just as Peter said, soldiers were gathering behind some of the large hydraulic machines.

There, buried against the far wall, was a metal room. Audrey could see it clearly. It must have been the hidden room. Audrey looked at Peter. He nodded and put a finger up to his lips to be quiet.

A few dozen men with blast sticks guarded it. For a while, they were placing dark grey boxes around the room.

After a minute, Audrey heard a rusty squeak. Now, a strange looking shadow stood just inside the open doorway.

The shadow looked like a man, but he was hunched way over. His clothes were ragged and torn. His arms were very skinny, and he had long bendy fingernails. They could also see tuffets of odd-looking wiry hair.

Audrey looked at Peter, puzzled.

*Who is that?!* she wondered.

The shadowy man motioned for four guards to step inside the doorway. Then, the same four guards stepped back out. This time they were walking with a stretcher. Someone was lying on the stretcher under a heavy white sheet. Everything was filled with such mystery!

Audrey stared with her mouth open.

The guards turned away. They were heading back toward the Center, but by a different route. Marching off, the whole group of guards began to disappear.

As they got further and further away...

...as the last little glimpse of light faded...

...and as Audrey could almost see nothing at all...a robot arm fell out from under the white sheet!

"There's a robot under there!!!" Audrey squealed!

"Hush! They might hear us!" Peter barked.

Sure enough, a couple guards in the back spun around. They stared toward Peter and Audrey, and after a second, the two guards began running back.

"You two, what are you doing there?!" they shouted.

Audrey watched Peter panic. Peter rustled through his pockets.

"I've used up most of my gadgets in the scrapyard." he said quickly. "There isn't much left. All I have is a long pipe full of fine ash. It would be good to blind one person, but not two! We should go!"

Audrey didn't wait. She started to run behind Peter. They tried ducking in and around the hydraulic machines. It was too late! The guards split up. Soon Peter and Audrey were trapped in a narrow passage, with one guard on either side.

"What are you kids up to?" They held up their blast sticks. The tips started to glow in a scary way. The narrow passage grew faintly green.

"Hey! Why are you two Pickers here?!" Someone else was yelling.

Audrey was stunned.

Linda came barging around the corner. "You lousy Pickers! How many times have I told you not to wander off! Now I find you a mile away from the Center!" She tore into the narrow passage and shoved the first guard out of the way. He bounced off the hydraulic machine and rubbed his forehead.

All the while, Linda continued screaming at the top of her lungs, "How dare you both! Oatmeal for a week! Pot scrubbing for the next month!"

Peter and Audrey were frozen. Linda just yelled and yelled and yelled. Audrey was dumbfounded. Linda knew she wasn't a Picker. Then when the time was just right, Linda winked at them both! Audrey smiled. Linda wasn't here to yell at them. She was here to save them!!!

Linda continued her pretend tirade with a secret smile, "You lousy excuses for no-good Pickers! You're gonna drag every pot to one side of the cavern and back! I ought to do worse to you!!" She grabbed Peter and Audrey by their ears and began dragging them out of the narrow passage.

Somehow her yelling was even louder than the whirring hydraulic machines! When the guard tried to stop her she even turned on him! "How dare you?! How dare you point blast sticks at a couple lost kids! Morticia will hear about this! Do you know who I am?!! I am a Lead Picker! How dare you both?!"

"Umm...umm...I'm sorry, ma'am. We didn't mean anything!" the guard stammered, "Th...th...there's no need to report anything. You can go."

"I oughta..." Linda twirled a fist in the air. "...but I won't, for now!" She turned her head back to Peter and Audrey and stormed off. "C'mon you two! Let's go!"

Audrey put on a great show. She sighed. She cried. She even, *Why? Why? Why'd?!* – until Linda's ears felt totally fried!

Audrey kicked and yelled. She and Peter pushed and shouted – until they were all very far away, and then they fell over laughing!

The three rolled around in the middle of an empty neighborhood. Homes sat quiet around them as they laughed and laughed.

"I can't believe you shook your fists at them!" Audrey snickered.

"I can't believe they were stuttering!" Peter laughed so much he could hardly breathe!

Linda sat up first and smiled. Still on the ground, Linda propped herself up by putting both hands behind her back. She had a look of thought on her face.

"I'm proud of my acting," she said, but then Linda appeared sad. Her eyes reddened, and she bit her lips to stop herself from crying. Linda admitted, "I wasn't really acting. I talk that way, most of the time. Corrine was the only person who had the courage to point it out. In a strange way, it means Corrine was a better friend than anybody."

Peter and Audrey sat up too after a while. Both of them leaned forward and hugged their knees.

After a while Linda spoke, "I think I made a mistake. Morticia called me into her office last week. 'Jasper is the one to blame', she said. 'No one would have gotten hurt if the ban had been listened to.' She said he was *permissive*. That means to allow something bad to happen for a long time. Morticia said Corrine's death was Jasper's fault too. There is supposed to be a funeral. Corrine will be buried right after Jasper's trial. She said she wanted to stop the violence, and she told me to warn the Rockets. She wanted me to tell them that the Hurricanes were planning something terrible. I went to Aaron, and he blew up. After I thought about it, I realized Morticia doesn't want to end the violence. She used me. She wants us fighting, and she's going to blame Jasper for everything. If the gangs destroy each other, then there's less work for her to do. I shouldn't have gone to Aaron."

"You didn't know, Linda. Morticia used you. I don't believe anything that woman says, especially about Corrine. It's gonna be okay. Maybe we can find Aaron and the Rockets before something bad happens." Audrey said warmly.

"You're being too nice to me. I'm sorry I told you to scrub the pots."

"That's okay." Audrey smiled. "I know your job is hard. Maybe if we agree to work together, we can become friends."

"Friends?" Linda looked like she didn't believe Audrey for a second.

No one liked Linda. Everyone knew that. Audrey could tell that Linda thought that maybe Audrey was making fun of her, the way the other kids did when she was little.

"The older kids used to mess with me. They called me *squinty*,"Linda shivered.

Audrey sympathized with Linda. She obviously hated that word. Linda didn't trust people easily.

"You're not messing with me?" Linda asked, suspicious.

"Not at all!" Audrey answered.

Audrey was unique. People just loved her warm smile.

Linda said, with an air of caution, "Well...maybe."

Audrey grinned from ear to ear. She placed a hand on Linda's arm. "It's a start," she said.

Both girls looked at Peter. He was deep in thought. Rubbing his chin, he said, "Now we have two more mysteries. What was that thing under the white sheet? And who was that creepy shadow? We have to find out about both!"

"Peter, we aren't going back there! We just got away!!" Audrey pleaded.

"Audrey, we have to! We have to be brave, for Corrine and Jasper! The mystery has to be solved! By now, the guards are all gone. Linda, will you help us?"

Audrey thought for a moment. If they got caught, they would be in big trouble. She could lose her position as Planter.

Linda sighed and admitted, "After Corrine yelled at me, I talked to my dad. He misses my mom a lot. She died many years ago. I was too little. I don't remember her, but I have her picture, and I look at it every day. My dad said that he remembers a little girl helping in the Infirmary. She stayed by my mom's side every night. They became friends and she helped my mom a lot. My dad described the girl. He said she was short. She had beautiful dark skin, and braided knots along her head."

"Corrine!" Audrey knew it was her.

"I'm not surprised." Peter rubbed his chin. "We've learned a lot about her. Did you know she's been in the Province from the beginning?"

Linda added, "What Corrine said was a message from my mom. It was my mom who said, 'Tell her I love her. Tell her how much she meant to me!' Corrine was there, and she hasn't aged!"

Peter stood up and announced, "We're gonna solve this together! Audrey and I are going back to the hidden room. Linda, can you follow the guards with the stretcher?"

Audrey looked worried, but she shot Peter a slightly brave smile. Audrey knew Linda was scared, but she was still ready to try.

"I'm on it!" she said. Linda shot to her feet. Her thick glasses slipped off her nose, and she pushed them back up. She looked around hard and squinted her eyes. Linda placed both fists at her hips and demanded, "So, which way did they go?!"

Peter and Audrey giggled. They both pointed toward the Mecca. At the same time, they cracked wide grins and blurted out, "That way!!!"

## Chapter 18

### The Creepy Man with White Wizened Hair

Peter led Audrey back to the hidden room. Like Peter
guessed, by now all the guards were gone.

The twosome passed the whizzing and popping hydraulic
machines. Quietly, they crossed the long part of the cavern
too.

Peter pointed to where he glided before. He was up among
the highest stalactites. Audrey looked shocked, and her
mouth formed a big capital O, as if to say Woah!

"You were so high!" she said in amazement. Audrey held
both hands up to her eyes like binoculars. She spun in circles
and pretended like she was flying too.

Peter turned red for a few seconds. "C'mon, silly head!" He
smirked and then dragged her along.

After scouting ahead, they tiptoed up to the secret door.
Everything was quiet. Peter could see tons of guard footprints
in the dirt, all leading away now.

It seemed safe, but there was still the problem of the creepy
man. He was in there, somewhere.

Peter felt like his heartbeat could be heard far away,
although he didn't want Audrey to know! He imagined the
men in Machine Town standing up and wondering what that

sound was! Peter felt like his heart was as loud as a giant stomping around.

Peter put a finger up to his lips. "Shh!" he said, more to himself, as he tried the handle.

Sure enough, the door creaked a lot. Peter turned the handle slowly. He wanted the squealing metal to be as quiet as possible. Thankfully, the door opened, and no one was waiting for them on the other side.

The hallway was empty.

Peter remembered sneaking down here a couple weeks ago. The dark stairs smelled musty and gross. Drippy old copper-water lined the sides of the hallway.

It was very dark. They could hardly see!

As Peter and Audrey ventured forward, every little sound made Audrey jump. They were like two little mice scampering along. Carefully, they crept down the hallway into an open laboratory.

Dust covered groups of old beakers. Test tubes and glass coils were on every table, and computer and science books were everywhere!

Peter could picture what the room must have been like a long time ago. He got very excited. There was so much to learn here! Clouds of blue and green, colorful liquid shooting through glass tubes, and bubbling beakers filled his imagination. He could see fizzy puffs from neat chemicals and dozens of scientists working side by side. They were doing experiments! He even imagined they were solving the problems of the earth. They were looking for a way to melt the ice, everywhere!

Now their knowledge was all forgotten. Peter grew sad. The beakers were unused. There were no bubbling chemicals. Even the books waited for nobody.

What a waste this room was! Why did they abandon it? He rubbed his forehead.

*No!* he thought. *This can't be! Something needs to be done!*

Peter watched as Audrey crossed the room. She walked up and down the long tables full of tools. She clearly had never seen anything like them before. Most of the tools weren't even made of copper! They were made of some kind of shiny white metal.

This whole room held one mystery after another!

Then, they both made their way to the back of the room. Here, the real adventure began.

The entire back wall was covered in parts for robots. There were arms, legs, eyes, and parts of their brains! There were special computers and silver tables too. The tables were designed to fit a robot, half-inside. It was like one of them could lay down and fit perfectly into the table. Cables ran from the computers to the table.

Audrey strolled up to the table. She ran her fingers along the smooth surface.

"No dust..." she remarked to Peter.

Peter cursed himself. He should have noticed that! The table was just as she said, clean and well-used. The room had been used a lot recently, but not for science.

Next to the table was a computer, and this one was turned on! The green screen read: *Locate all files?*

They both leaned in.

Someone had typed in the word: *Yes*!!!

Peter clicked the keys. This computer was way more advanced than the ones he had at home. It was like the big computer in the Center. Peter had built his from scraps and leftovers from the old world, and he had found a few old books on programming. This computer was completely different.

"There's nothing here," he said sadly. He couldn't find out anything more.

He tried and tried, but there was nothing to learn.

Worse yet, as they studied the monitor, a spooky face began to appear in the reflection. There was someone right behind them! Suddenly, the person grabbed Peter and Audrey by the scruff of their necks!

"What are you two doing here?!" a creepy old man barked.

Peter and Audrey screamed.

Quickly, Peter grabbed the long pipe from under his jacket. It had a narrow blow hole in either end. Each side was covered by rubber corks. In a flash he yanked out the rubber corks, put it up to his mouth, and blew hard. Black ash flew out in a tornado.

A huge cloud of soot covered the old man's face. Surprised, he dropped Peter and Audrey and started coughing and wheezing.

The twosome started to run, but then they skidded to a halt.

"Drat! Drat! Drat!" the creepy man muttered loudly, "Oh my, my, my, Morticia will be so angry." He started to weep. Something was actually nice about his voice. He sounded rather harmless.

Audrey stepped forward, "It's alright. We won't tell her."

"You won't. You won't? You won't!" The creepy man said with three different tones. He dropped to the floor in relief.

The creepy old man looked so funny sitting in a heap. He was covered in soot, dirt, and old soiled clothes. He wore a thick pair of goggles too. After he pulled them off, they could see his eyes underneath. His left eye looked nice. It looked at them with a kindness to it. But his right eye was crazy! It spun around in an angry circle! It even glared at them from time to time. The creepy old man smiled, sort of, but only out of the left side of his mouth. The right side wore an angry frown.

Abruptly, the old man started flopping his white wizened hair about, trying to shake off the ash. He wore a long set of overalls and no shirt. He was bone skinny. His arms and legs were wiry, and he had a strange spunky bounce whenever he jumped up.

"Now I'm so happy!" He slapped his own forehead a bunch of times. "I was afraid you would tell her that I couldn't dig far enough!"

"Dig?" Audrey asked sweetly, "What do you mean, dig?"

"I tried. I tried to find the files, but I couldn't. Not this time. I dig for computer files. They bring me that funny robot sometimes, and I dig. Dig! Dig! Dig! That's what I do! There's so much, and they're so deep. I can never dig far enough. All I can do is bumble-jumble the funny robot." He blurted out quickly.

"You're Mortimer, aren't you?" Peter remarked.

"Yes, Mortimer! That's my name! That's what they call me!"

It was Audrey's turn to frown. "Wow! I thought he was a myth!" she said.

"So did I," Peter whispered.

"Morticia sends the thing to me, and I dig, dig, dig. Ha! Ha! Ha!" Mortimer said.

Grabbing tuffets of his long white hair, Mortimer pulled it painfully into two clumps on either side. Strangely, he sort of steered himself by turning his hair. Mortimer leapt over to the monitor.

"Ahh!!!" Mortimer suddenly screamed. "I forgot a whole bunch!!! I didn't erase everything! Morticia's gonna be angry. It's your fault!" He accused his own reflection, and banged his head off the screen. "Look for the files. Dump! Dump! Dump! We don't want to hurt the Province. Robots are bad!"

"What robots?" Audrey demanded.

"All robots. Bad robots. Worse robots. They're all dangerous!" Mortimer jumped onto the table and glared at them from overhead. "Why?!"

Audrey stumbled back while Peter stood firm.

Mortimer continued, "Do you know any robots?"

"No," Peter said truthfully. "We don't know any robots."

Mortimer started dancing on the table while singing the words, "You don't know any robots! You don't know any robots!!!" His skinny legs kicked back and forth.

"He's crazy!" Audrey nearly shouted in Peter's ear, while sort of whispering, "My belly is doing flip-flops. I want to get out of here!"

"I know. I think there's something here to learn, however," Peter said. "I just can't figure it out."

"Morticia is wonderful!" Mortimer sang. "Wonderful! Wonderful! Wonderful! She brought the foul thing to me, and I dug further than ever. I dug into its head til I thought it was dead. There was nothing left. Then I found more. There was something deep inside. It has such a strong core! The computer in the Center, that's what I need. I'll find out what it knows. Erase! Erase! Era...! Hey!" Mortimer's right eye abruptly stared at them. "How did you get in here?" He asked like he had totally forgotten. "Did you come in with that foul

robot? Trouble, it is. Don't listen to it! It doesn't like
Morticia! Now, get out! Get out! GET OUT!"

Mortimer picked up a glass beaker and hurled it at Peter.
Glass shattered onto the floor with a crash. Mortimer grabbed
another. One by one, Mortimer started throwing everything
he could get his bony fingers on.

"I don't like you two! Down into the Dungeon we go if you
don't leave. Leave now! Now! NOW!"

Audrey didn't need any more reasons. "Let's go!" She yelled
and took off down the hallway.

Peter wasn't far behind.

Out of the hidden room, they ran, down the hallway, and
out the door. Grabbing the handle, Peter pulled hard.

Somehow, even though they ran far away, Peter thought he
heard singing again from deep within the hidden room.

It all happened so fast.

They ran and ran and ran...

...and neither of them gave another thought to the dark
grey boxes. As the kids ran off, all the boxes began to tick.
Then an eerie whirring came from inside, as did an odd green
glow.

Chapter 19

The Stranger in Black

Peter led the way as he and Audrey walked back toward the Center.

"Over here! Hurry!!" Linda barked to Peter from behind some barrels.

Peter and Audrey hurried over and just in time. A second later, two of Morticia's guards walked by.

"What are you doing back here?!" Audrey nearly shouted.

"Linda's hiding, silly!" Peter frowned. He then laughed and shook his head.

"Something huge is going on!" Linda remarked. "Morticia's guards are looking for us; that's right, US!" she explained to Audrey. "...you, me, and Peter! I think the two guards that we fooled reported back, and now Morticia knows we've been snooping around. Captain Rodney keeps storming around too. Everyone is afraid of him. That's for sure. His stomping shook the whole ground!!! I've never seen him grumble so much! He's looking for something else. He dug a weird grey box out from behind a meat stand! Then he marched right up to Morticia's office! Morticia's in the Center, and Rodney knows she's not in her office! So why did he go to Morticia's building then? A lot of people are talking about it."

"Slow down!" Audrey squealed. "Did you say *grey boxes*?"

"We saw some of those back in the hidden room..." Peter added.

"Guess what?" Audrey cut him off. "Mortimer is real! We ran into him! He was *sooo* creepy!!!"

"You met Mortim...!!!" Linda almost screamed.

"Will you two be quiet?! There are guards everywhere!" Peter pointed.

"You're right. I'm sorry," Linda apologized.

For a moment Peter was shocked. Linda had never apologized before. Peter turned his head to the side.

"It's okay," he said. "We're friends now, you know."

Linda pushed up her thick glasses and turned beet red. Quickly, she started nodding and added, "I love you guys! I really always did. I'm sorry I've been so mean."

Audrey's mouth dropped! So did Peter's! They both grinned from ear to ear, but before they could say a thing, a strange sound rang out. The sound was very loud, like a cave in – crumbling rock and twisting copper all at once.

In a snap, Peter whipped his telescope goggles on.

"There's a person on the other side of the Mecca," he said. "Someone or something just broke through the dungeon's door. The wooden door is totally shattered with some of the stone wall too!"

Peter scanned the Mecca. He focused his goggles. His vision shot past all the people and stands, over the bridges, and beyond the narrow stone streets.

"That's where Rodney's building is. It's where he trains Morticia's soldiers," Linda explained, after figuring out where Peter was looking. "It's where they brought the stretcher. That's why I'm here. This is as close as I could get. You don't think the thing on the stretcher broke free, do you?"

"Only a robot could break a dungeon wall like that," Peter answered. "Whatever it is, it's heading for Morticia's building."

*** 

Rodney stode into Morticia's building.

He was tall and fearsome. The Captain of the Guards was so big. He carried *two* blast sticks, one in each hand! Rodney also had a grey box under his arm.

Pushing his way down the stone hall, he searched and searched.

Morticia wasn't here today. She was preparing Jasper's trial down in one of the squares. No doubt she was shaking her head, grumbling, pointing, and giving orders. She was probably wondering where he was.

He didn't care.

Rodney's nose snorted like a bull! He was very upset. His heavy boots stomped through the building. As he reached the top floor, he noticed a woman standing in the doorway of Morticia's office. It was Maureen.

Rodney put his blast sticks down at the end of the hall. He pulled his heavy black gloves off and dropped them too. Rodney's thick fingers formed lines in the air as he walked over.

"Jasper right. Morticia losing her mind. I found these bombs around the Center. Maybe there are more around the whole Mecca!" Rodney signed as he opened the box.

Maureen peered inside. The box was made of the same parts as a blast stick. The middle glowed green. There were other parts too, like a radio. Maureen looked up, shock dripping down her face.

"These are bombs!" she agreed. "What is Morticia trying to do?"

"She angry when I let the kids go. I think she means to kill us all, me and you. I think she wants to start over," Rodney explained with sign-language.

Maureen rubbed her chin as she worked it out. Rodney watched her. She walked slowly over to the window and thought. Rodney patiently waited until she talked.

"She's done this before," Maureen said. "When I was a child, she wiped out the whole Province. I thought she was protecting us. Most of the adults followed Professor Franklin across the ice. It was a mistake. They left too early. Many didn't return. When Morticia's parents died, something inside her switched. She took charge of the Province and tore the Lift down. Life began over, like the above-ground never happened. She wanted to ignore the old world, and she made us forget the ice. Everyone accepted our new home down here."

Maureen continued, "Then, ever so slowly, Morticia got rid of everyone who remembered. The older people got shipped far away. They died over time. The last adults were no match for her new army. I didn't stop Morticia, and look what happened. Corrine's dead."

"I never forgot your parents. We never forget Corrine," Rodney signed, as he smiled.

"I've done all the wrong things, Rodney. I was protecting myself."

"We all afraid of Morticia," he answered honestly. "I a coward too. So we fix it. We must stand together, with Jasper."

"If we question Morticia; we question the whole Province. Will they listen?"

"We try! Morticia asked me to bring the girl from the fields – Linda. Morticia spreading rumors that Cutter planning something big. I bet Morticia told Cutter the same thing about Aaron. Morticia the one fueling the gangs against each other."

Maureen began figuring it out, "Rodney, we have to save the Province from Morticia. She'll blame Jasper and the gangs for the bombs. If they all die, Morticia can restart the Province. Almost everyone is gathered in the Center. She's going to set off the bombs today!"

"The jumping gangs at Daggers Hollow too!" Rodney added quickly. "The two gangs supposed to meet now. Gonna be a big clash! Bombs probably there too."

"Daggers Hollow would be an ideal death trap. It's going to end with a huge bang!" Maureen nodded and continued, "There will be no one left to ask questions. Can this really be happening?" Maureen started shaking her head. "Would she be willing to kill us all? Would she kill a bunch of innocent kids?"

"She would. These bombs the proof." Rodney looked terribly sad. "Bombs all over the Center. She has her own army. A few still loyal to me. We check the rest of the Mecca. The kids at Daggers Hollow need to be warned. She wants to get rid of everyone, including you. Bombs all over this building too. She asked you to come here, didn't she?" he signed.

"Yes," Maureen whispered in horror. "She said this would be the best view of the trial."

"Morticia's madness has gone too far. In her mind, she will do anything to rule the Province. We all in trouble. Maureen, will you help me?!" If Rodney's signing could have been heard, it would have bellowed loudly.

Maureen nodded. She was starting to cry. Rodney knew this meant that everything would change for her.

"I betrayed the whole Province," Maureen sobbed. She wiped her cheeks off again and again. "I betrayed Corrine. She thought she was s-safe. She thought I was okay to talk to, and I wasn't. I-I wasn't a good friend. I thought I was protecting Corrine, but I was just another tool for that woman. I was a spy for Morticia. Now Corrine's gone, and I have no way to say I'm sorry..."

Rodney put up his finger to stop. His hair was standing up on the back of his neck.

Maureen wiped the tears from her cheeks.

Carefully, they turned around.

Down the other end of the hall, another person was listening! It was a stranger! Neither Maureen nor Rodney had seen them before!

The stranger was wearing all black. They had black pants and a black hoodie, covering their face! Somehow the stranger had already stolen Rodney's huge gloves and his blast sticks!

This person could have slipped away easily, but they didn't. For some reason, the stranger was listening to Rodney's conversation, and they were crying too. Something Maureen said touched the stranger greatly!

Rodney acted quickly. He went to take a step, starting to storm down the hall, but the stranger was much faster. Before Rodney could even move, the stranger whipped the blast stick up. Faster than a rabbit, they fired overhead.

Rodney grabbed Maureen and shoved her into Morticia's office to protect her. His choice was smart but useless! The stranger wasn't aiming at either of them.

Instead the fiery green glob flew toward the ceiling. One by one the lights shattered! Glass and sparks rained upon the hallway. It grew dark.

Standing in the dim lighting and shrouded in a shower of sparks, the stranger glared at Rodney.

Despite all his strength and training, Rodney stayed put!

Fire rained down between them both. For a minute, they stared at each other in the darkness.

Then the stranger turned and thrust a fist right into the wall. Somehow, the wall blew into pieces!

Even Rodney was shocked. How could anyone have power like that?

Then, Rodney got his answer. Just before the stranger leapt away, just before they shot him a final glare, and just before their shadow disappeared through the gaping hole and dust, Rodney saw a metal arm.

Chapter 20

Danger at Daggers Hollow

Linda, Peter, and Audrey snuck up to Morticia's building.
Peter took the lead. As soon as they got there, the upper wall
blew out, right above their heads!

Then, the strange person from the dungeon jumped out of
the hole and down, almost thirty feet! The tiny person wore
black from head to toe! The stranger ran along the rooftops
toward Machine Town and Daggers Hollow beyond.

Peter watched the strange person through his goggles. The
two girls had a hard time keeping up, so Peter grabbed their
hands and pulled them along.

He kept yelling, "Over here!" and "Over there!"

All three of them had to tear through backyards and
alleyways just to keep up!

Finally, after a lot of running and a monstrous amount of
huffing and puffing, the threesome reached Daggers Hollow.

They had a hard time seeing over the crowd. The Rockets
and Hurricanes were very far away. It was hard to push
through all the other kids.

Audrey kept jumping up to get a glimpse. But the stranger
was nowhere to be seen.

"I don't think either team has spoken yet!" Audrey
announced.

"It doesn't matter," Peter reminded her. "We're here to find that strange person. Keep your eyes open."

Audrey nodded, as Peter turned his attention toward the seething crowds.

The tension was high!

Word spread fast amongst the underground kids.

Most of the Rockets were Planters, and the Hurricanes were mostly Miners. The team's rivalry would clash today!

Kids from all over the Province gathered together. There were hundreds of them. One group after another snuck under the Falls to see the battle. Daggers Hollow was no longer a secret!

Clusters of jeering kids pushed and shoved. Everyone wanted a glimpse. The whole cavern hushed when the Rockets finally arrived.

The Rockets walked tall and proud. As they strode into Daggers Hollow, a large open gap formed.

Then, everyone's head turned. Slowly, they heard the sound of a drum. It was deep, and it bellowed loudly.

Thump-Thump. Thump-Thump.

The heavy rumble grew closer.

Thump-thump! Thump-thump! — Thump-thump! Thump-thump!!!

All of a sudden, the Hurricanes marched in. They looked fearsome!

Cutter walked in front. His skin was pale, and his hair was carved into a mohawk. He was tall and lanky, and his outfit was dark silver. His muscles were long and thin, but he still looked strong.

Cutter had nine others with him too, ten people together.

Since the tryouts never finished – and Corrine vanished – Aaron had only nine Rockets.

As soon as the Rockets and Hurricanes entered, the crowd pulled back, opening up some space. Both teams stood on either side of the open gap. Now, they stared each other down...

*** 

Deep in Daggers Hollow, on the other side of the crowd, Aaron wasn't afraid. He took a few steps forward.

Cutter did the same. The young team leader walked up with a sneaky sneer on his face.

Both teams likely brought weapons. Cutter did a sort of spin on one foot and opened his arms wide. He was trying to show that he had no weapon, that he meant no harm, but Aaron wasn't stupid.

"You're planning something," Aaron accused him strongly.

"Maybe." Cutter studied Aaron. "Word in NewTown is you're the one with the problem! The streets are buzzing with talk!"

"Enough with the buzz. I heard things. You heard things. It doesn't matter," Aaron answered. "Now, what to do about it?"

"My thoughts?" Cutter slyly rubbed his chin. "Let's call it final. I'm tired of fighting teams. No more yearly games. Let it be decided now who rules. I say we run the pit, and whoever lives keeps everything."

"Is that a threat?" Aaron said, as he took another step forward.

Cutter said "whoever lives". Aaron was bigger than Cutter, but Cutter was a fast fighter. He stared Aaron down.

"It's a fact. You're not good enough to make it past the pit," Cutter answered with a smooth voice. "Let's do this. No tricks now."

Aaron glared at him. There was nothing to trust about Cutter.

The crowd started to cheer. This was going to be the best show they had ever seen – both leaders facing each other down the gauntlet.

Aaron had no idea what Cutter was planning. He strode confidently up to the edge and began stretching.

When they were standing off to the side, the tall Asian Rocket walked up and warned Aaron, "He's up to something."

"I know, Kojika," he said. "There's nothing I can do about it. He has to be stopped here and now."

"Walk away," Kojika pleaded.

"No one will join our team again. I can't show weakness. If I don't face him alone, both teams will kill each other. He wants to handle it between us, and I'm going to bring it!!!" Aaron's face was like stone!

"Then be careful," Kojika nodded. "Stay focused. Don't blink. Keep your eyes on the course, and just try to finish first."

Aaron knew this race wasn't about finishing first. Cutter didn't want him to finish at all!! Still, he knew Kojika would worry. Aaron winked at her and smiled for a moment. With that, he walked away. Standing at a distance from Cutter, Aaron stepped up to the edge.

As he did, the whole crowd shifted. Everybody wanted to watch. Both team leaders were about to jump the "pit"! There was no hard floor here. There were no bumps and bruises. This was the real deal!!

Part of Daggers Hollow had a flat floor. That's where all the kids were gathered now. The rest was quite different. At the edge of the crowd, Daggers Hollow plummeted for hundreds of feet.

There were all kinds of stalagmites. Sharp spikes rose up all over the place. Over time, the jumping teams had worn some of them down. There were key places where you could land. There were others where you couldn't. Some routes to the other side were easy. Some were hard. One route – called the "pit" – was nearly impossible.

It's exactly what Cutter wanted. Aaron knew Cutter had snuck in and practiced here before...

\*\*\*

The rooftop stranger knew danger was coming fast. The stranger's sharp eyes got a first glimpse through the crowd. The stranger was looking for something else.

Dark grey boxes were everywhere. No one else noticed them. Most of the kids were jumping up and down shouting with glee.

Studying the ground along the wall, the stranger spied twenty or more grey boxes on each side. Quickly the stranger worked, gathering up armfuls of boxes – bombs – and dumping them near the middle.

Everyone was focused on Aaron and Cutter. They never paid attention to the stranger slipping in and out of the crowd.

## Chapter 21

## Surviving the Pit

Far in front, Aaron and Cutter took off. The crowd roared!

Aaron landed first. He was fantastic! His jumping wasn't like Kojika's. He leapt strong and proud. With strength he hit each of the platforms. Launching powerfully, he was soon off and onto another.

Cutter was great too. His body was more flexible. He spun head over heels and made his way upward. Cutter was climbing.

Aaron wanted to gain distance. All he wanted was to get to the other side. So he wasn't paying as close attention, and Cutter's trap was laid.

At a certain point, Aaron ran out of places to land. There was a huge hole in the stalagmites ahead. He paused.

Cutter turned and softly whistled.

One of the Hurricanes shot a hateful look at Kojika. This boy was even taller and skinnier than Cutter. The skinny Hurricane grabbed something from behind.

Before anyone could stop him, he threw a large copper sword. Reddish light gleamed off it brightly as the sword spun through the air. It whipped around and around.

Ever ready, Cutter was waiting. Grabbing the sword roughly, he nearly tore it out of the wind's hand. Then, he turned a set of dark eyes toward Aaron.

Kojika screamed. She leapt toward the pit.

Knowing the trouble it would cause, the other Rockets stopped her from stepping in. Most of the Hurricanes jumped forward too, itching for an excuse to fight. No one was allowed to join Aaron's and Cutter's battle. If Kojika tried, so would the others, and more, and more, and more. Nobody would stop the violence then.

Quickly, one of the Rockets handed her a set of small "jos". A jo was a thin copper rod. These two were tied together with a ribbon. She grinned from ear to ear. If Cutter was allowed a weapon, why not Aaron?

"Aaron!" she yelled.

Aaron spun around.

High above, Cutter was crouched like an animal. He was ready to attack. Sure enough, Cutter leapt. The team leader hollered. He had a high-pitched voice! Cutter focused on Aaron.

Just in time, Kojika threw the copper jos. They flew straight and fast. Aaron grabbed them, tore off the ribbon, and held them up...and not a second too late! Cutter swung the sword down, and Aaron blocked it with a clang!

The force of Cutter's sword was very strong. Thankfully, Aaron had a jo in each hand. Cutter's sword was sharp, but Aaron had two copper rods!

Cutter landed with a thud. He swung the sword again and again.

Aaron stumbled back. Rather than fall, Aaron took another step and jumped. There was a small place to land nearby. Aaron jumped again, this time to a larger platform. He ducked low and paused.

Cutter wasn't far behind. His teeth were bared! Spit ran from his mouth, he was so angry!

Aaron was ready. He jumped up and swung both jos. Cutter had to move fast to block both. Somehow he managed to.

Aaron swung over and over. Cutter swung again and again too. They both jumped and jumped. Cutter even chopped down some of the stalagmites. Aaron too wanted to slow Cutter down. Sometimes he slammed both jos into a platform. The stone crumbled under his strength. Now the "pit" was harder than ever.

Almost on the other side, Cutter swung his sword fiercely. Aaron jumped too. The young men smashed together in the air. Their weapons clanged! Their bodies thudded against each other.

Landing hard on the far floor, they had made it! Both team leaders rolled to their feet. Neither knew what to do. Now they were separated by a few meters. Both had landed at the same time, and there was no clear winner. They looked each other in the eye. Both Aaron and Cutter were breathing heavily. Aaron gripped the copper bars tightly. So did Cutter with his sword.

The only thing left was to continue to fight. Cutter's eyes thinned. He wanted more...

\*\*\*

During the fight, the stranger watched the crowd with narrow eyes.

The crowd oohed and ahed! Many had both hands alongside their cheeks. The girls squeezed their eyes shut whenever Cutter swung. His sword was so big and scary! Shiny sparkles of red light reflected around the cavern.

Cutter wanted Aaron dead, and so when they landed together, the crowd went silent. The cheering, the oohs and aahs, and even the squealing girls stopped. The resounding battle in Daggers Hollow fell to a dead quiet.

Suddenly, a blast of green energy shot from the middle of the crowd. It was aimed straight at the other side. The green ball flew toward Aaron and Cutter, but it didn't hit either team leader. Instead, the green energy sliced through the air, right between them.

It exploded on the far wall.  Crackling oozing goo hissed and popped.

Again the stranger shot a blast from the center of the crowd, and again it flew between the team leaders.  It was so close!  Aaron and Cutter backed away from each other.

"Stop!!!" came a tiny yet powerful voice!  The voice sounded mechanical.  It was like one of the hydraulic machines and a person was mixed together.

The Hurricanes, the Rockets, and everyone else turned.  The whole cavern stared at the person in the middle.

The stranger was wearing all black.  They had huge black gloves and a black hoodie.

No one could see who was underneath.

The stranger stood alone in shadow, crouched low with two blast sticks.

The crowd stepped back.  So busy were they, watching the fight, that they didn't notice this person laying out the grey boxes.  There was a pile of boxes on the stranger's right and another pile on their left.

The stranger wasn't wearing anything from either team.  They weren't one of the Hurricanes.  They weren't one of the Rockets.

"Why are you fighting?  Do you believe lies?!  Morticia has lied...to you all!  You are...pieces...in Morticia's game!" the stranger asked.

"What do you know?!" the tall skinny Hurricane argued back.

The black clothed stranger reached over and grabbed one of the dark grey boxes. Hurling it over the edge, the crowd stared as the box fell below and exploded! It exploded with so much force that gusts of wind whipped over the side.

Even more of the stalagmites collapsed. Like thunder, the cavern rocked as the mighty stone spikes crashed into each other.

The stranger's voice spit out confusing sounds and garbles, "These are... her bombs!!! Daggers Hollow... was to be your tomb! Why do you fight each other!!! Take your fight... to the Center... to Morticia. Killing each other... solves nothing. Join... together!"

The tall skinny Hurricane walked forward. He wiped black soot off his forehead. The kid was frightening, but he was also trying to make a point.

"We know the Province is in trouble," he said. "All the miners live on scraps. We live in dirt and sooty homes. Somehow we survive. Miners are friends with nobody else! Farmers are only friends with farmers. Planters are only friends with only planters. It's the same with Machine Town. Every corner of the Province fights for itself! That's how we live! That's how we survive."

"Join the jumping...teams...together!" the stranger pleaded again. "Speak as one voice! Together...Morticia will listen...to the Province!!!

"You want us to gather the whole Province. You're asking us to do the impossible. What makes you think Morticia will listen?"

In answer, the stranger quickly aimed their blast stick at the grey boxes. The tall and skinny Hurricane stumbled back. He looked like such a coward.

***

Standing off to the side, Kojika smiled. She only knew one person this brave. She was starting to figure it out. She knew who the stranger was, but then her stomach sank.

The only way to gain the respect of the crowd was to do the impossible. And the pit was ruined now...

*No one can handle this part of Daggers Hollow! Not even you! Not even me!* Kojika thought.

Knowing what the stranger was planning, Kojika started to scream, "Noooo....!!!"

She never finished.

***

Suddenly, the stranger bolted forward. Their black hoodie flapped in the wind. Then, the stranger ran up to the edge and leapt high over the crowd. Ramming the blast stick on the ground, the stranger used it as a pole vault!

As the stranger soared up on high, they also spun around to face the cliff's edge.

Everybody was staring.

The stranger fired their blast stick toward the edge. A dozen times they shot! With a loud crack, the rock started to give. Huge boulders began tumbling as the floor gave way.

The crowd stumbled away. They backed up to safety, further and further back.

Suddenly, the whole floor along the edge fell into the Hollow. Tumbling with the rocks and stones, went the dark grey boxes! Morticia's devices all fell far below. Just before the stranger landed, the cavern floor, hundreds of feet below, exploded. The ground shook and rumbled, but the mightiest stalagmites stood firm. Green fire spread across the bottom of Daggers Hollow.

Rushing up to the new "edge", the kids watched in terror as the stranger jumped and jumped.

Many times the stranger used the blast stick as a pole vault, springing from one platform to the next. Sometimes there was only enough space to put one foot down! Sometimes there wasn't even that! Sometimes they swung off a sharp spike, or spun in circles, and at the right time kicked with both feet.

The stranger didn't care how difficult it was. They needed to prove that the impossible was possible!!!

\*\*\*

Audrey spotted Kojika. The tall Asian Rocket had tears in her eyes, actual tears! Kojika was even smiling! Audrey carefully walked over.

"Why are you crying?" she asked with a soft tone. "Who is that?"

Kojika's head turned in slow motion. Kojika answered just as softly, "Can't you tell?"

Audrey turned back toward the stranger. She saw the way they moved. This person was an artist. Audrey saw their graceful movements, beautiful spins, and perfect gentle landings. Audrey's eyes opened wide, and she too started to cry.

\*\*\*

A glimmer of green light bathed the stranger. They made one death defying leap after another. The person jumped further than anyone ever had. They spun in circles and twirled in spirals.

Somehow, they did all that while aiming the blast stick. Two...three...four...five shots rang out. Then they turned and kept shooting – ten...twenty...fifty times – more than anyone could count. The stranger aimed and fired so fast! Each grey box blew up with a poof and a boom!

Madame Morticia's plan was to blow the boxes up at once. No one would have survived. Separated, the smaller explosions weren't very powerful. Now the stranger had destroyed all the bombs – while jumping!

Through the darkness the stranger jumped. Through the most dangerous, the seemingly bottomless, the scariest, and through the hardest course in the Province, the stranger leapt!

With a commanding thud, they landed on the other side.

To the shock of the crowd, to the surprise of Aaron and the other Rockets, the stranger tore back her hood.

Beautiful African hair shimmered in the dim light. Corrine stood tall and proud!

The whole cavern erupted in cheering!!! All the kids jumped up and down!

Audrey, Peter, and Linda were all crying tears of joy. They hugged each other in a group and even jumped up and down too.

Everybody was so happy.

Somehow, Corrine made the impossible possible. She saved all their lives. Now, she leapt in a whole new way.

Corrine had leapt through their imaginations and into the very hearts of all.

Then, Corrine went even further. Tearing off her right glove, she exposed a robot arm for all to see. Holding the blast stick high in the air, she looked back and forth between Cutter and Aaron. Corrine's metal fingers gripped the staff firmly!

"She will listen!" Corrine announced. "She will listen to ME!!!"

## Chapter 22
## Corrine faces Morticia!

The courtroom was dim.

Madame Morticia sat on a high bench. She looked very serious! Along the bench were a few Overseers. The other people inside the courtroom talked for hours.

After a long time, Jasper was led in.

This trial was very strange. A dull whisper grew in the room.

The guards pushed Jasper up toward a long empty table facing the bench. Roughly, the guards forced him down into a chair! Even though it hurt, Jasper didn't flinch.

Morticia looked like she had just eaten a rotten apple. Hatred filled her face. She sniffed at him.

Two hundred people from the Province filled the courtroom. A couple hundred more were stuffed into the courtyard, just outside, and at least two thousand people surrounded the courtyard in the whole Mecca!

Guards were everywhere. They looked tense!

"Jasper." A grey haired man stood and spoke. He was a fellow Overseer, and yet Jasper's name oozed out of the man's mouth. "You have been accused of crimes against the Province. You have acted against our laws! You have disobeyed our orders!  And worse, you have insulted and questioned our very leader!!!  What do you have to say?"

"Honorable Overseers," Jasper said with a cool tone. "It is not the Province which I question.  The Province and the people are dear to me, but the place I call my home is in trouble.  A dangerous rat has slipped in!  We have been misled!  This woman, Madame Morticia, needs to be seen for what she is!"

"How dare you?!" The grey haired Overseer shot to his feet.  Throbbing veins abruptly bulged out of his forehead.  "Madame Morticia had provided everything for us!  Why, from the time I was a child she was there!  It was she who held the Province together!"

"Here, here!  Here, here!" The other Overseers banged their fists on the long bench.

They all agreed.  Things were starting to look bad for Jasper.

Morticia smiled and nodded.

"Let me explain," Jasper tried to reason. "Madame Morticia is hiding the truth about a special young girl.  I combed the whole Province in search of her.  For a while, I felt like I was chasing whispers.  Rumors told the tale of a broken girl.  She lived in lost caves, talking to herself.  The stories from the older ones went as far back as the Province itself.  So I asked Morticia...

"I made myself an enemy that day," Jasper went on. "The Overseers began to ignore me. Morticia said "no" to everything I asked for. But it doesn't matter.

"Somehow, the broken girl found me! A month ago, I found some files about her on the Center's computer, very large and hidden. As I studied the special passcode, a silly girl came bouncing along. Her name was Corrine, and she danced around me for almost an hour. She was funny, goofy, and stubborn. I was so annoyed! This silly young girl talked and talked. She had ideas about planting. Corrine rambled on, about plants, soil, water, leaves, fruit, and vegetables – while twirling!!! All I wanted was to be rid of her. I almost screamed.

Jasper went on, "Corrine knew all about planting, but she didn't know why. Then, my mouth hit the floor. The secret person I was looking for was right in front of me.

"There's something Morticia isn't telling us. It's time to leave the Province. The Province creators hid a device above ground. It's called the Earth Engine. The Earth Engine can save our planet. Corrine knows about it and how to use it to reseed the world. All of the information, Corrine's hidden files, were sealed by a man. The secret to fixing the earth was placed inside his creation - inside Corrine. Corrine is a robot, and Morticia has been working to bury our knowledge of her. I heard the man's name before, the one who sealed the files, when I was a boy. It was Professor Franklin!"

The courtroom gasped. People started shifting in their seats. They looked back and forth and whispered loudly. Some started yelling either "Lies!" or "Guilty!". Then, they raised their eyes toward Madame Morticia and the other Overseers. Everyone wanted to know what would happen next.

Madame Morticia laughed. She actually laughed in Jasper's face!

"Professor Franklin," she said while shaking her head, "what do you know about him, Jasper? The man was crazy! Everyone knows the story. He led our parents, his friends, out onto the ice, to their doom!!! Most of them died. What happened to poor helpless Corrine? She's dead too, because of you! It's your fault! These are nothing but stories from a frightened man. You're trying to distract us. Humph!!! You're guilty, Jasper. You have spoken against the government! No one in this courtroom believes this nonsense!!" Morticia lied through a pure white smile.

The people believed her. More than one threw trash and pieces of apples at Jasper. Groups of Miners grumbled loudly. The Machinists hurled hateful words at him. Even the adult Planters looked angry and threw vegetables!

Jasper sat in his chair and didn't move.

Morticia smirked proudly. She faced the Overseers and went on, "Do any of you believe him – secret files – a magical Earth Engine – a robot girl? Preposterous!"

The Overseers looked nervous. No one wanted to speak against Morticia. They were all afraid. Jasper watched them, and he felt bad for them. They would never grow. They would never be better.

"Then I say, Jasper, you are guilty!" Madame Morticia said sharply, "Jasper, you are hereby removed as an Overseer! You will be treated as the worst of criminals. Into the mines you will go. You will wear soot all the days of your life. And oatmeal is all you will ever eat!!!"

Jasper started to rise off his chair. Slowly, he stood. Four guards grabbed him around the arms. Still, he rose. Jasper wore copper chains and handcuffs, and somehow he still looked so cool!

"Is Corrine dead?" Jasper asked.

Morticia stuttered for a moment, not knowing what Jasper meant. His tone suggested that he wasn't really asking the question.

"Remember this day, Morticia," Jasper went on. "For it is the day you lost. It is the day everything and everyone crumbled from your fingers! They won't believe me. They *will* believe her!!!"

Suddenly, a strange sound grew from outside. The whole Mecca was in an uproar. People miles away were screaming. The strange noise grew closer and closer. It was a deep thunderous sound!

The courtroom stared. Everyone was pushing and shoving to get a glimpse. When they turned to face the windows, the noise got even louder!

Suddenly, hundreds of kids raced into the courtyard! The courtroom doors burst open! Kids poured into the trial! They were jumping off the chairs, off the tables, and even off the walls! Windows shattered as more kids rushed in! The Hurricanes and Rockets led the charge!

"Shoot them, you fools!" Morticia ordered.

"Madame Morticia!" Another Overseer, a woman, tried to stop her. "They're just kids!"

Morticia didn't care. "Shoot them all!" she yelled.

The guards responded quickly. Green energy exploded around the room, but this time the kids were moving too fast.

Jasper never budged. He never took his eyes off Morticia.

Morticia could see her trial falling apart. In a panic, Morticia grabbed at the nearest guard. Tearing his blast stick away, she shoved him aside. In anger, Morticia raised the blast stick toward Jasper.

Abruptly, to the surprise of all, another figure leapt into the room. Morticia froze. Out of all the kids, this one stood out as amazing! The person was dressed in all black. They jumped in a perfect line, straight from the door, down the middle of the courtroom, and up over Jasper's head. They jumped so high and so gracefully! With a slam, they landed on the table in front of Jasper.

Again, Corrine tore her hoodie off.

"Impossible!" Morticia's mouth dropped.

The whole courtroom froze. Everyone stopped. Even the guards ceased shooting to stare!

Corrine thrust a clay pot high into the air. Inside was a plant no one had ever seen. It was beautiful! The plant had long green leaves and a dozen purple flowers. They were long and elegant!

"T-t-this is called an "Iris". It fell-fell from the Column!" Corrine explained. Her hands were shaking, and her voice was garbled with marbles. Still, she tried to speak, "The ice-ice isss melting! O-o-our earth is growing again! It is tim-time to return!"

"No!" Morticia shouted. "You little snake! The earth isn't safe. Everyone knows that!"

"Your reign has-has ended!" Corrine answered. "The earth *is* ready ag-again. I-I-I should have known! Never trust an ugly bun!"

"How dare you?!!!" Morticia howled!

She raised the blast stick. Morticia fired a huge green glob straight at Corrine. It flew through the air at lightning speed!

Corrine didn't move! She stared Madame Morticia down. Corrine's eyes shimmered angrily in the fiery green light as the blast sped toward her. Then, at the last second, Corrine threw up her other hand, and caught the green fire!!! She snatched it right out of the air!!!

Corrine looked at the ball of energy sizzling in her metal hand! As the liquid green fire dripped between her fingers, her eyes flashed back toward Morticia.

Morticia's mouth hit the floor; so did the whole courtroom's!

Morticia's face twisted. She looked angry and mad. She looked nervous and sad, but something else was brewing. Suddenly, she looked sneaky and glad.

Madame Morticia pulled one of the radios from her pocket.

Corrine gasped. It was a controller. Morticia probably put grey boxes all around the courthouse!

The woman Overseer marched over. "How could you, Madame Morticia? You could have killed her. She's just a young girl! But, then, she isn't that young, is she? You did lie to us. You lied to us all. We've been breathing coal dust for years and dying. Have you no pity?"

Morticia sneered.

Without even looking, Morticia placed a hand on the woman's face and shoved her away. "This Province is mine!" Morticia ranted. "I built it!!! We were happy without you! I told Maureen you were nothing but trouble! Ha! Now, you'll go down with everyone else!!!"

Aiming the radio at Corrine, she pushed the button with a wicked grin.

Morticia's controller sent out its deadly signal with a zing! There was a distant boom, and another. The room began to tremble. It shook, shimmied, and shuddered! Some said it even shivered! Suddenly, small stones began to fall from the ceiling.

Corrine winced. Was the building going to collapse in on them? Something was wrong. The explosions sounded like they were very far away. She waited. So did Morticia. After pieces of the ceiling hit the floor, a shower of dust floated down.

That was it.

Corrine opened her eyes. She let out a nervous breath and looked at Morticia.

The woman wore a bigger and more confused sour frown than ever!

Then a large shadow formed in the doorway. The whole courtroom backed away as General Rodney stomped in. Audrey, Peter, and Linda were behind him too. Rodney's arms were full of dead bombs. All their wires were pulled out.

Then he spoke! He actually spoke!

"Morticia!" His voice boomed, deep and loud! "In the past I saw so many die that I could not raise my voice anymore, but now I must! These are your people! What have you become?!!!"

Morticia's face turned beet red. "Those bombs weren't for you!" She lied.

"Weren't they?" Rodney saw straight through her.

There was to be no fibbing here!

"We found where you hid them all, Morticia," Maureen announced as she stepped into the courtroom behind Rodney, "around the Mecca, your own building, and here at the courtroom. Even the bombs at Daggers Hollow are gone now. You meant to kill us all! We moved the bombs far away from the Center."

Rodney's voice shook the stone tiles! He continued, "Is this how you reward the Province? All these people worked hard for you. Now you want to tear it all down? Why?!!"

"Without me there is no Province!" Morticia lost her temper. "I built it! I saved it! When the adults left us behind, I carried you! I fed you. Everyone who left froze and starved. It was that robot's fault!" Morticia aimed a bony finger at Corrine.

"Corrine isn't to blame!" Maureen argued, "Franklin knew he was getting old. It might have been a mistake, but he didn't have a lot of time left. Others chased that dream with him. They knew it might be too early, but they made a choice!"

Morticia argued right back. "Franklin thought the earth could be rebuilt. He was wrong! Corrine didn't have the answers then, and she doesn't now. They followed that robot to their doom, and the dream died with him!"

Maureen pleaded, "Corrine saved some! She saved my parents. She helped us find the survivors. Her beacon led us to them! Don't you remember? Her beacon signaled: 'Help us. We need help.' If she hadn't done that, more would have died."

"My parents didn't survive! It's her fault, and there's nothing you can say that will change my mind! That flower proves nothing! The sunshine and trees are never coming back!" Morticia screamed.

Morticia threw her desk over! It landed with a loud thump.

Under the desk was a hidden hole! She was so crafty! Morticia shot her blast stick along the ground. Flames exploded between her and the crowd. Green fire formed a ring around her. No one dared to step close. Morticia's face and hair shone brightly!

Just before jumping into the hole, she cackled, "I built this place. I'll tear it down! I'm tired of you, Maureen, always protecting Corrine! You're all going to pay for it...

...and if you won't stay, I'll make sure you never leave!!!"

## Chapter 23
### Remembering the Dolphin Clinic

Corrine started shaking as the last of her energy drained away. It took so much strength to face Morticia. Her voice was getting worse, and her body crumbled underneath.

Corrine fell to one knee and then off the table!

Just before she hit the floor, Jasper jumped in and caught her. She felt terrible. She wanted to scream. She wanted to cry for help, but nothing worked. Her arms were frozen. Her mouth was jammed shut. Everything was growing so dark!

"Corrine!" Audrey yelled and ran over.

Corrine's mind was all jumbled. She strained to remember why. Then a memory flashed through her head..it was of Mortimer!

\*\*\*

Mortimer found Corrine at the bottom of the deep chasm and dragged her through abandoned tunnels for miles.

Corrine was barely awake. After what felt like forever, he pulled Corrine inside a steel door. It was the back entrance to Professor Franklin's lab!

Mortimer turned the rusty handle, and inside they went. Then creepy old Mortimer flopped Corrine up onto a table. He grabbed a long cable and shoved it into the side of her head!

Corrine could hear whirs and pops. The computer was making noise. It beeped and bopped! Then a whole bunch of computer files came up on the screen.

"What do you mean, NO?!" Mortimer screamed at it. "Dig, dig, dig, that's what you need to do! Delete the files!" Mortimer hit the computer again and again. He was so angry!

Corrine lay still. She had no fight left in her.

The computer tore her memories apart. The machine dug into her mind and wiped her dreams away. She couldn't remember anything!! How many times did Mortimer do that to her? Five? Ten? A hundred? She could recall his ugly face and bulgy eyes! How much did he take? This was all Mortimer's fault! Or was it?...

\*\*\*

*Those were my memories!* she yelled inside. *You had no right to take them!*

That's why she wasn't working right!

"Mortimer...cable...side of my-my-my head..." she mumbled to Audrey.

"Mortimer?!" Audrey screamed. "He did this to her!"

Peter bounced over. "It all makes sense! Mortimer must have found Corrine after she fell! Corrine was the 'robot' he was talking about. He said, 'Morticia sends the thing to me, and I dig.' They must have done this to Corrine every time!"

Jasper shot a hateful glance at Maureen and said, "Look at what you allowed!"

"I'm so sorry," Maureen whispered. "I thought we were protecting the Province."

Audrey's bottom lip quivered as tears welled up in her eyes. Then, she wiped them away furiously. "How could you?!" She faced Maureen. "She was your friend!"

Maureen knelt down. "I'm so ashamed. I was told that Corrine's memories threatened the Province. At first, we only erased her memory of Professor Franklin and the lab. Then it came back, faster and faster. Corrine spread ideas about leaving. We were afraid more people would freeze to death. I was wrong. I didn't mean to hurt Corrine. I was too weak to face Morticia."

"Look at her! You fed her to Mortimer! You did this!" Audrey screamed. She was right.

It was Maureen's turn to cry. Gobs of thick water dripped down her cheeks.

"It's...okay..." Corrine took Maureen's hand. She looked at Audrey and Jasper, and then at Maureen. "Morticia...has ways...striking...fear! I forgive you. ...friends?" With that Corrine's eyes rolled up. Her body went limp.

Maureen couldn't take it anymore. Nearly throwing up and bawling her eyes out, Maureen pushed through the crowd and fled from the courtroom.

"Corrine..." Audrey turned back and grabbed her friend. She looked at Peter. "She's getting worse. Can we fix her?"

Peter thought for a minute, tapping his feet on the ground. Then his eyes shot up to Jasper's. At the same time they both said, "The computer in the Center!"

After that, the whole room fell into a frenzy. People were running around. Peter and Jasper ran off to fetch the computer.

Rodney stormed over to Morticia's guards. Rodney didn't have a weapon. There were fifty guards, each had a blast stick, and yet they were all afraid of Rodney! He tore the sticks from their hands!

"You work for me now!" he bellowed. "Your punishment will be to serve the Province, for the right reasons! I will train you, and it will NOT BE PRETTY!"

By the time he finished screaming, they weren't Morticia's guards anymore.

The other Overseers were shouting orders too. Someone called for a cart with wheels. Another group opened a gap in the crowd outside.

Corrine could hear it all. She was having a hard time. She couldn't separate what was happening now from the things that were a memory...

***

She could see the old lab in the dome. Mr. Franklin was very young. There were people and robots working together there too.

Some of the robots were good. Others weren't. The bad ones were planning something terrible. She was going to have to fight. She had planned the whole thing out. Beneath the ground it would have to wait. It was the only way. Inside Professor Franklin's computer, she wrote a secret file. It would worm right into the heads of those terrible robots!

Corrine would have to be patient. She was just a simple program right now, Professor Franklin's new idea. She could see the lab through the computer camera, but she didn't even have a body yet. She watched the scientists all day. And she watched the robots all night...

***

Peter and Jasper rushed back into the courtroom. They had a huge miner's pushcart! They pushed and shoved real hard! Inside the pushcart was the computer from the Center. They grabbed everything they could think of! They had boxes of parts, and heaps of wires.

Peter quickly jumped into action. He ran cords and cables. He pushed buttons and computer keys! After what felt like hours, a green light came up on the screen. The crowd cheered! Peter felt awesome!!

Carefully, he felt along the side of Corrine's head. There he found the spot he was looking for. A small round connection was hidden off to the side. It was made for a cable! Peter found what he needed in his box of copper wires.

*Yuck!* Corrine thought. Her mind floated in a milky sea. *I SOOO HATE COPPER!*

Peter pushed the wires into the side of Corrine's head...he put the other end into the back of the computer...and the computer went simply crazy!

The screen turned from green to blue! A huge amount of data started to fly across the screen. The computer was working on something huge...

\*\*\*

Corrine heard voices, far away.

Starlight spirited her journey.

She was floating. There was nothing else around, only the distant heavens. Then she saw it, a faint light, and the faint light was a room. She swam closer. When she opened her eyes, she was standing on the far left of a familiar room. She was in the Dolphin Clinic.

Professor Alexander Franklin walked over to the whiteboard. It was covered in lots of math. Graphs, symbols, and numbers were everywhere. He shook his head. The math was very troubling.

Another woman walked up with a clipboard. This woman was Indian and so pretty. She had dark hair and red horn-rimmed glasses, and she looked very smart. The woman waited for a moment. When Mr. Franklin noticed her, she walked up to him.

"There's still a chance?" she asked hopefully.

"No," he answered firmly. "The earth cannot be saved. We have to form another plan."

"What are you suggesting, Professor?" The Indian woman put the clipboard down, pushed up her glasses, and folded her hands.

"Charmaine, I named this "The Dolphin Clinic" for a reason. The majestic creatures look up and leap high out of the ocean. They dare to dream! Dolphins also know when to dive deep. This is one of those times. We need to bury the Earth Engine. What we need is an ark."

"What do you mean?" Charmaine tilted her head to the side. She looked very curious.

"We need to find a way to preserve our memory. The most important data – our books, literature, history, stories – needs to be saved. I think we need to build a robot."

"A robot? You've tried this before."

"Yes. I made mistakes with them. This robot will be better in every way. That's what makes her so special. Her core memory will be the strongest computer ever invented. Inside this robot is a key. She will wait for many years. After the earth freezes, she will be able to restart the Earth Engine. Only then will we be able to stop the people who pushed the freeze into motion."

He went on, "She will make mistakes and will have failures, but she will learn and grow like a human. She will feel tired, pain, and sorrow. Her heart will ache, but she will know joy and love too. She will not just be alive; she will live! Through it all, my robot will develop a personality of her own. Picking ourselves up and trying again are the keys to becoming great! Over time, she will be better and better!"

As they talked, the two scientists strolled across the room. It was bright white. There were desks and chairs in the room, like a classroom. Everything was shiny and clean. Sunlight streamed in.

On the far left side, a silver robot was standing alone. They walked up to it.

"It's going to take a long time to build. Thankfully, this is only a dream."

"What do you mean?" Charmaine asked, rather upset.

"I'm sorry, Charmaine. Both you and I are long gone. This robot was my greatest creation!"

Wind built up in the room. The wind was cool and refreshing. Starlight and heavens began to spin around the robot. A twinkling shower fell upon it. The robot began to have fingers and toes. Beautiful dark skin and pretty clothes grew onto the robot.

"Corrine." Mr. Franklin knelt down in front of her. "When the time is right, you will see the first natural growth. That green means the earth is fighting to survive. I've placed the Province in an area that will begin melting first. If there are other humans, they may not have much time. You can save them. Inside you are instructions which we need to regrow. The Earth Engine has a device which can start the melting. It has packs of roots, stores of pollen, and lots and lots of seeds. You need to open the door. When you see new plants, go to the Earth Engine!"

The wind spun around Corrine in a beautiful array. Flowers blew in and surrounded her. Sunbeams, pink petals, dewdrops, and brilliant green leaves all spun together! Corrine lifted her big brown eyes. She was shining!

Mr. Franklin spoke louder and louder. His voice got prouder and prouder. "You will have emotions. You will create, uplift, and unite! You will dream, imagine, believe, aspire, and soar! You will lead us back home!"

Then he began drifting away. The room faded, leaving only white behind.

Corrine reached out and warmly whispered, "Goodbye, father."

"It's time to wake up, Corrine!" Professor Franklin whispered from far away, "It's time to leave!!!"

\*\*\*

The courtroom jumped away.

Numbers, and diagrams, and codes flashed by on the computer monitor! The screen sizzled and popped! The computer even began bouncing around inside the cart! Yellow sparks poured from the cables all around the room. All of a sudden, the lights went out. Everyone stood in pitch black, wondering what would happen!

Peter leaned forward.

Blue light shot from Corrine's eyes! Then, more blue light sprang from her fingers, her mouth, and even her ears! Her body lurched and stretched in funny ways.

The whole crowd was stunned! Everybody's mouth dropped open, even Kojika's!

Abruptly, Corrine sat up.

The blue light started to dim.

Peter fell back. So did Jasper, Maureen, and Rodney!

Then Corrine slowly stood up. She was facing away from the whole room. Computer codes and lost memories flooded in. Corrine felt like her head was being put back together.

She stretched her hands and legs.  Looking down, Corrine
spread her fingers apart, and then she formed a fist.

Corrine turned back around.  Now she faced the room.

Looking at her friends, Peter, Audrey, and Linda, she said
loudly, "We have to go!  Now!  There are more bombs!
Morticia is going to blow up the Column!"

## Chapter 24
### Friends Together Again!

There was no time to wait!

People joined in, by the hundreds, to follow the new Province leaders. Jasper headed the march. With Rodney by his side, no one questioned him now!

After watching the crowd for a while, Corrine started to lag behind. She grabbed her head. It hurt so bad. Chunks of memories swam around her. They were like suitcases in a rushing river. She reached and reached, and they floated away. Sometimes her fingers could grasp a latch, and one would snap open. The more she thought, the more she remembered.

Little pieces from last week floated in. She remembered the games. She remembered jumping, climbing to the top of the wall, and falling. She fell and fell.

*How did I survive?*

The answer lay right before her. She looked at her nimble fingers and saw metal. Her skin must have torn when she fell. A normal person would never have survived.

Corrine raised her arm high into the air and studied it. Slowly, she pulled her sleeve back. Metal ran down her whole arm. Her shoulder, her elbow, her wrist, and even the tips of her fingers were shiny silver.

Neat white cables ran along her arm too. Energy ran through them, not like electricity. This energy glowed slightly blue as she moved. The cables flexed and stretched. They were so cool! She wiggled her fingers. Sure enough, they moved and felt the same.

The computer from the Center was Professor Franklin's, and it helped to rebuild her mind. Corrine knew the truth now! It was time to go back to the Earth Engine. She was supposed to save everyone, but then, another memory haunted her. It made her cringe inside and crumple outside! She folded her arms tight. She wanted to go back home. She wanted to crawl into bed and hide from the whole world!

Audrey ran over. "Are you okay?"

"No," Corrine muttered quietly.

"What's wrong? You can tell me!" Audrey wore a smile. She was carrying the flower now. Audrey made sure to keep it safe.

"What's going on guys? Is everything okay?" Peter hopped on over too.

"Professor Franklin made me," Corrine explained. "He said I needed to save the world."

"Is that a bad thing?!" Audrey squealed.

"Are you kidding?" Peter asked with a frown. "That's awesome!"

"Audrey..." Corrine whispered. "I wasn't good enough. I let you fall."

Corrine looked up. The adults would describe her face as "anguish". She felt sadder than she ever had. Corrine could feel her eyes fill with redness, and drops of water were about to tumble down her cheeks. At the same time, she felt strangely serious. Corrine wanted to pull away and hide her face, and she was worried that she was neither good enough, nor strong enough, nor brave enough. And the Province needed her. She was in terrible pain, defeated, worried, and nervous at the same time!

"When I woke up at the bottom of the chasm. I thought you died, Audrey! I was too weak to fight Mortimer. He dragged me across the cavern, and I cried and cried. You fell, Audrey, and it was all my fault! I didn't deserve to be rescued! What's the use of these stupid robot hands if I cannot save my friends – and if I cannot save my friends, how can I save anyone else?"

"I'm not listening to any of this!" Audrey yelled at her. "Nobody's perfect! Not even you! You have robot arms, but you don't have eyes in the back of your head! Tell me! How were you supposed to know that a guard...like...I don't know...a mile away...shot his blast stick in the wrong direction? Tell me!"

"I...umm," Corrine stuttered.

"You don't know, do you?" Audrey challenged her. "Corrine, you're amazing! People around you want to be better, because of you! They fight for you now! Everyone is here for you! You *are* going to save the world! Don't you see? There's a reason you know so much about planting. You were made for this!"

"You should have seen the way you jumped across Daggers Hollow," Peter explained. "Everybody was in shock! You united the two gangs! Even Cutter was willing to listen! You gave Jasper the courage he needed. It was all you, Corrine! There's a reason I call you 'Core'."

"I thought it was just a short way of saying my name," Corrine was confused.

"No silly!" Peter burst out laughing. "I call you 'Core' because your heart is so strong! You are warm and kind. You are funny and goofy! When we need it, you are so brave! Your 'core' is beautiful!"

Corrine burst into tears. This time, they were tears of joy.

"You guys are amazing too! Audrey, you always make me feel better when I feel the worst, and Peter, I don't know who could save the day better than you! I love you guys! You are my sunshine, my joy, and my breath!"

"Aww!" Audrey squealed. "Those were my mother's words!"

The three friends wrapped each other up in a giant hug.

"Come here, you!" Corrine addressed Linda.

Linda ran over too and hugged all three. She was so happy she picked them all up, right off the ground!

Corrine felt good about the battle ahead.

Now they were united.

Now they wore a strong look of courage!

Finally, they were ready to face Morticia!

***

Morticia pulled the lever hard. She was fuming! This was the end! If they wanted to leave, she wasn't giving them the chance!!

She combed the caves under the caves. It took a long time to find Mortimer. Then, the brother and sister walked briskly through the underground tunnels. Mortimer kept seeing dumb things and wandering off. She rolled her eyes and dragged him along. They argued and bickered the whole way!!

After a while, she found an old abandoned tunnel! It was ancient and spooky. This tunnel was right under the Column! She hadn't been here in years. There were giant gears mounted to huge pipes! They reached up very high! Also there was a small lift. It wasn't like the one she tore down all those long years ago. The larger one was just huge. It could carry an entire hydraulic machine from the surface all the way down!

Morticia and Mortimer climbed into the small lift car. She pulled the lever, and the lift started to rise. Slowly, it creaked toward the ceiling! As it got close, the elevator forced its way through the ceiling. Morticia had all of this sealed years ago. Now the elevator pushed toward the very cavern where the Column was. Dirt spilled away from the top of the elevator, drilling away above Morticia's and Mortimer's head. Then, Morticia's elevator burst through!

***

Corrine could see Morticia as the elevator rose, very far away. She watched Morticia study the cavern.

To Morticia's horror, the green glow from a blast stick lit up the darkness. Then there was another, and another, and another. There were ten, then fifty, then hundreds. Her mouth fell to the bottom of the lift! A quarter of the Province stood side by side, together against Morticia. Corrine was so proud!

Rodney stepped forward, next to Corrine.

"It's over, Morticia!!!" he bellowed.

"End this madness!" Corrine shouted. "Where did you put the rest of the bombs?" She flashed Mortimer an angry glare.

"Here, there, and everywhere!" Creepy Mortimer answered with super sneaky glee.

"What do you mean? I told you to put them in a circle, '...at the bottom of the Column.' That's what I said!" Morticia argued with Mortimer.

"Hee. Hee. Hee! I wanted to surprise you with presents!" Mortimer chuckled. His nice eye looked admiringly at Morticia, while his angry eye cast evil glares at Corrine. "I made thousands of bombs, more bombs than you could ever ask for, more, more, more!! They're hidden around the big drippy pipes. They're in the hallway. They're even up on the sides of the Column! I put them everywhere!" Mortimer danced in the elevator. "Just aim the remote, and they'll pop, pop, blow!"

Morticia grinned.

She aimed her remote control toward the guard's hallway. Pressing gently, she carefully set off one of the bombs. The ceiling just above Rodney, exploded.

"Back off!" she ordered. "I have the power here!"

Dirt and rocks showered down on the crowd, just behind Corrine. Many screamed and started to flee.

"Morticia!" The woman Overseer from the courtroom started to speak.

"No more talking!" Morticia cackled.

Morticia aimed two more explosions near the outer wall.

More dirt and large rocks tumbled down. The crashing sound was so loud! It was hard for Corrine to see and breathe.

"I'll bury you all!!!" Morticia laughed and laughed, while Mortimer danced and danced.

"Bury the robot! Bury the robot!" Mortimer mimicked her.

"Yes!" she agreed, rubbing her chin. "Back away! All of you! Get out of here or this cavern will be your tomb, everyone except Corrine! Corrine stays behind!"

"What do you want with her?!" Audrey shouted with courage.

"Let's go!" Jasper grabbed Audrey. "We can't win this if we are all dead!"

"No!" Audrey kicked and screamed.

"Jasper's right!" Peter yelled. "Morticia is too far away! She can blow up the entire room!"

"Go!" Corrine said to Audrey. "We can't stop Morticia this way. She's gone from crazy-pants-crazy to utter madness!" Corrine agreed with Jasper.

Still, Audrey struggled and fought. Jasper pulled her along, as the rest of the crowd and the Overseers backed out.

The entire crowd fled down the guard tunnel, the same one that the two guards were using when Corrine and Audrey took the flower.

Morticia laughed more as she aimed the remote along toward the tunnel first. More bombs exploded and more boulders crashed down as the guard tunnel collapsed, sealing Corrine in with Morticia and Mortimer!

After forcing everyone else out, Morticia faced Corrine. The little robot bravely stayed behind. It was the only way to protect her friends.

"Now for you! You robot pest! I should have destroyed you years ago. Why did I ever listen to Maureen when she kept telling me to keep you around? Let this be a lesson to all! No one defies Morticia!" the mad woman screamed, as she waved the remote around, pushing the button at every bomb beneath the whole Column.

Bombs all around Corrine exploded one by one. Morticia cared about nothing as long as the Column was destroyed and Corrine along with it. Huge amounts of stone caved in and down upon the small elevator, as the earth buried Morticia and Mortimer in an earthen tomb.

Tons of rock cascaded toward Corrine! Hurling herself toward the secret tunnel and the drippy green pipes, Corrine slid across the floor. But she was a moment too late.

As she skidded into the secret tunnel, the largest pipe of them all fell.

Corrine looked up just in time to cover her head as it crashed down upon her!

\*\*\*

Hundreds of people ran for their lives away from the Column. Cracks formed along the guard tunnel's wall. Pipes began to fall overhead.

Jasper let Audrey down.

Audrey could hear one loud boom after another from the cavern behind. Morticia must have been destroying everything! Now Audrey knew why Jasper had to grab her. Morticia was indeed crazy-pants-crazy!

Hundreds of Province citizens streamed out of the guard tunnel toward safety, and not a second too late.

For a few minutes, the ground heaved and rumbled! Then, a burst of dusty dirt blew upon them.

The Column had fallen.

The quaking was over.

Shaking herself off, Audrey wiped grime from off her face. Abruptly, she realized something. She had forgotten about the secret tunnel! Maybe Corrine found a way to escape!

"Cmon," Audrey said to Jasper, Maureen and Rodney. "I know of another tunnel!"

There was not a minute to waste.

Audrey began running, in and around a hundred homes and through several caverns. She ran all the way to the entrance of the secret tunnel, but when she got there, and when Jasper caught up, Audrey looked at him with her bottom lip quivering.

The secret tunnel had caved in too.

"Not to worry, my dear," Jasper explained, as many people from the Province began gathering behind him, wheezing from their hurried run. "Did you know I saw her this morning? They brought Corrine into the dungeon. She had fallen a couple hundred feet. Mortimer found her and drilled into her head. When she woke up in the cell next to mine, she couldn't even remember her name! She was broken, but she didn't stop. Even then, Corrine wouldn't give up! Guess how she got out?"

"How?" Audrey wiped her face on her sleeve.

Jasper leaned over and whispered into her ear.

Audrey started to giggle as a broad smile spread across her face!

Jasper began explaining, throwing his fists forward, and describing how Corrine had shattered the very stone!

## Chapter 25
### Saving the Province!


On the other side of the tunnel, Corrine awoke with a start!

She was pinned under the pipe. She couldn't see. She couldn't hear. She wanted to cry, but soon she remembered Audrey's words. She was going to save the world! No crazy mad woman, no bombs, no cave-in, and no pipe was going to stop her!

Corrine got madder and madder. She hated copper and avalanches! She hated scrubbing and...and Mortimer! She hated those awful blast sticks and...and...and Morticia!!!

Redness built up on her face. She was filled with fury!!!

"I hate copper!" she screamed. "I hate it. I hate it. I hate it!"

Corrine pounded her fist into the copper pipe. A terrible clang rang out. Startled, she pulled away. Her eyebrows jumped up, and her eyes grew large and wide! She looked down at her hand and back to the pipe. Buried within the copper was an imprint of a fist!

She felt her hand. It didn't have a scratch. Whatever she was made of, it was not only harder than stone, it was harder, stronger, and better than copper!

A narrow squint and a sneaky smile filled her face.

Corrine leaned forward. Driving her fingers into the copper, she tore right through it! With a loud grinding noise, she ripped her way inside the pipe!

Standing in the midst of a drippy green mess, Corrine got even madder...

\*\*\*

Audrey stepped away from the collapsed pipes.

"I think I heard something!" she said.

"What is it?" Maureen rose to her feet.

They could hear clanging coming from the tunnel. This was not a knock, knock, knock like someone would do to say hello. It was a strange sound, like the loudest bell. It got louder and louder, closer and closer!

Suddenly, the huge pipe blocking the tunnel broke open. Corrine stood in the hole! She pounded her way through the whole tunnel!

Jasper stared down the hole. He was startled to see she had broken a path clear to the other side.

"Come! Everyone come!" Corrine smiled. She wiped gooey green water off her face. "The Column hasn't collapsed, not all of it!"

Peter turned his goggles onto a high light. A wide bright beam lit up the hole in the drippy pipes.

Carefully, the Province picked their way back to the
Column. The Rockets and Hurricanes followed behind
Jasper, Maureen, Rodney and Corrine's friends.

Sure enough, a giant mound was piled high in the middle.
The cavern was ruined. New cliffs lined the sides. There was
no way to reach the top now. Everyone could see the bottom
of the Column, but it would take months to clear the mess and
rebuild the Lift.

As the massive cavern filled with people, Corrine ran to the
Overseers. She looked Jasper dead in the eye. "You are our
leader now! Let's work together! We're a team! Don't let
Morticia's tyranny rule this Province anymore!"

Jasper knelt down. "You didn't call us in here to see an
empty cavern. What are you thinking?"

"The Province needs to work together!" Corrine added.
"They need something to believe in! We are leaving today!"

"How Corrine?" Maureen asked. "How can we get that
high?"

"Leave that to me!" Peter started shouting. "You men over
there, start digging a hole on the top of the mound!" He
pointed to another group. "You men head to the Southern
Province. You'll find more bombs there around a hidden
room. They're hidden behind the large hydraulic machines
too. Bring the bombs here!" Still, he pointed to more and
more men. "You ten, get us one of the mining carts. You ten,
gather as many blast sticks as you can and find a rope! We

need food! We need warm clothes! We need backpacks! You ten..." He went on and on.

By the time Peter was done, the Province had worked together! They stuffed the top of the mound with bombs. Electric lines were run to them. Then they tied as many blast sticks as they could around the mining cart. That went on the top. Corrine, Audrey, Linda, and Peter gathered up supplies and climbed into the cart.

"Where do we go from here?" Jasper asked.

"Build the Lift again," Corrine answered him simply.

Jasper smiled. He knew already that they needed to rebuild the Lift.

"No Corrine," he said while gesturing toward the thousands of people filling the cavern. "Where do we all go from here?"

He wanted her to say something more, to the crowd. They needed inspiration and direction.

Corrine started to shake. She took a deep breath. There were so many people staring at her!

"You can do it!" Audrey whispered. "They need you!"

"Hey Corrine!" Aaron shouted, encouraging her. "Kojika and I are renaming the teams! From now on we will be called the Dolphins! In your honor!"

Corrine smiled from ear to ear! Yes! That was it! Dolphins dare to dream!

She took a deep breath and started talking, "NewTown was built by hundreds of dedicated men and women! Professor

Franklin was their leader. He was a great man! His Province was designed to save humans from the ice! And it has! It saved us all! It will not be known as "The Province" anymore. From this day on, it will now be called "The Preserve"!!!"

The crowd erupted in clapping and cheering.

Corrine wasn't done!

She went on, "Professor Franklin once said that majestic dolphins know when to dive deep. They hide under the dark ocean, but they also dare to dream! When the time is right, they look up and leap high into the sun. We have had to dive deep! For over sixty years we have hid in the darkness. It is time to return, and to rebuild, and to make a new home! Today, we are returning to the surface!!!"

The crowd just exploded! Everyone was so excited. Rodney wore a proud strong grin. Jasper stretched a fist high into the air.

Jasper kept cheering, "Yeah! Go Corrine!"

Maureen had rejoined them too. She looked scared until Corrine spotted her and smiled. Maureen grinned back and blew her a kiss. The woman was so short, she was jumping up and down because she was so excited and because she couldn't see! Her round face wore a proud smile. She covered her mouth with both hands and was crying tears of pure joy!

The once rival gangs now cheered together! The Dolphins would rise as the greatest jumping team in history! Aaron and Kijika kept shouting, "Yeah!!", whooping at the top of their lungs, and throwing their fists into the air! The whole Province celebrated!!!

Peter didn't waste a second. He rammed both fists onto a large blue button. Electricity shot across the room and over to the bombs!

"Get ready!" Audrey clutched the flower close!

Under the mining cart, the bombs lit! Then, at the same time, they erupted like a volcano! The mining cart was blown high into the air!

"Now!" Peter yelled!

All four kids switched the blast sticks on full! Green energy and smoke shot out pushing them even higher! Corrine smiled at Kojika and Aaron far below. The mining cart looked like a rocket!!!

"We're losing speed!" Corrine yelled as they approached the first ledge.

They quickly jumped from the cart to the ledge, and not a moment too late! The cart crashed back down to the big mound. The crowd cheered even louder as Peter, Audrey, Linda, and Corrine held their hands up in victory! They had made it to the top of the cavern!

"Where do we go from here?" Linda worried.

A sneaky smile flashed across Corrine's face. "We jump!" she said.

"I can't jump!" Linda started sweating.

Corrine didn't care. She laughed as she grabbed Linda's hand. Corrine's powerful robot legs coiled down, and then they started jumping together!

Linda screamed out of fear! She even covered her eyes with her other hand as they jumped and jumped!

Audrey followed closely behind. She could jump so well!

Peter too was jumping. He wasn't as good as Corrine or Audrey, but he did have wings! Peter pulled them out and sailed from one ledge to the next!

They jumped and jumped, circling the Column. The air felt clean and fresh. As they neared the top, none of the kids had seen such brightness! Sunbeams bounced everywhere, lighting their way! Around and around the Column they went, up and up, higher and higher! Until finally, they were out!

Corrine was the first to break through. She walked with so much courage! Linda bumbled her way up over the edge. Her eyes were wide and staring! Peter and Audrey bravely stepped up onto the surface too.

Ice covered most of the world. It stretched from one horizon to the next! Storms terrorized the sky. Grey swirls hurled themselves across mountains.

But there were also patches of green!

Near Corrine, small stretches of beautiful grass blew gently in the breeze. Wild flowers grew here and there. The sun was shining in places. The nearby ice was melting.

Corrine smiled.

She was as happy as she had ever been! They were home!! They were finally home!!!

And the best part...

...there was not a scrap of copper anywhere!